'What exactly are you suggesting?' Lisa demanded.

'I'm a wealthy man,' he said in a low voice. 'I already come to Melbourne quite frequently on business and I could come even more frequently for pleasure.'

'You make me sound like a fast-food outlet,' she hissed. 'Juicy steaks, medium rare, prepared to perfection while you wait! And a money-back guarantee if we fail to satisfy.'

Matt looked at her from under half-closed lids.

'Oh, I don't think you'd fail to satisfy,' he murmured.

Angela Devine grew up in Tasmania surrounded by forests, mountains and wild seas, so she dislikes big cities. Before taking up writing, she worked as a teacher, librarian and university lecturer. As a young mother and Ph.D. student she read romantic fiction for fun and later decided it would be even more fun to write it. She is married with four children, loves chocolate and Twinings teas and hates ironing. Her current hobbies are gardening, bushwalking, travelling and classical music.

Recent titles by the same author:

YESTERDAY'S HUSBAND
UNWELCOME INVADER
DARK PIRATE

MISTRESS FOR HIRE

BY
ANGELA DEVINE

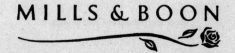

To my sister.

*MILLS & BOON and the Rose Device
are trademarks of the publisher.
Harlequin Mills & Boon Limited,
Eton House, 18-24 Paradise Road, Richmond, Surrey, TW9 1SR
This edition published by arrangement with Harlequin Enterprises B.V.*

© Angela Devine 1995

ISBN 0 263 79328 1

*Set in Times Roman 10 on 12pt
01-9512-55571 C*

Made and printed in Great Britain

CHAPTER ONE

'Tim!' shouted Lisa. 'Aren't you back yet? I'm getting a cramp in my shoulder!'

She raised herself on one elbow and gave an exasperated sigh. Even with the padding of a thick Chinese quilt spread beneath her, a dining table was not the most comfortable place to lie naked except for a thin drapery of silk. She twitched the green sari impatiently back from the curve of her hip, sat up and swung her legs over the side of the table. Luckily there were no neighbours who could look in, and the tossing green canopy of a silver birch tree produced exactly the quality of shifting greenish-gold light that Tim wanted for his study. It was to be called *Female Nude on a Spring Afternoon*, but as far as Lisa could see, it would never be finished unless Tim got out of the annoying habit of running out for a drink whenever his inspiration flagged. Suddenly she thought she heard the sound of a soft footstep downstairs.

'Tim?' she called hopefully.

There was no answer. Sighing again, Lisa rose to her feet and padded around the room. She had to admit objectively that it was in a bit of a mess, not that that bothered her or Tim. Why would any sane person want to have a dining room when they could so easily turn it into a studio? Oh, there were still a few signs of gracious living—the gold and white striped wallpaper, the cream Austrian blinds drawn up into opulent swags above the large picture window, a bowl of yellow roses that filled

the room with their heady perfume, not to mention the
Chippendale chairs pushed casually back against the wall
or the handsome mahogany sideboard that was almost
buried beneath the litter of paints, rags and brushes. Yes,
there were still a few faint indicators of the Lansdon
family's wealth and good taste, but on the whole the
room looked exactly like what it was. A work space for
two enthusiastic painters. And just at the moment Lisa
felt she would far rather be painting than posing.

She arched her back, trying to stretch the stiffness out
of her neck and wriggling her shoulders to loosen them.
What she needed was a really good work-out to loosen
her stiffness so that she wouldn't get pins and needles
and start fidgeting the moment Tim came back. Yawning
widely, she reached out one hand and put a cassette in
the tape recorder. Ravel's "Bolero"—now that was the
sort of music you just had to dance to! She began to
move voluptuously around the room, her back to the
door, letting herself sway and posture sensually with the
beat of the music. Anywhere else Lisa would never have
dreamed of dancing naked, but Tim was dedicated
enough to art to see her body only as an interesting com-
bination of planes and surfaces, even if he did return
while she was still in action. Ever since he had met Lisa
acting as a model in his life drawing classes six months
ago, he had regarded her as a cross between a great aunt
and guru. Since she was only six years older than him
this amused her, but it also made her feel safe. Safe
enough to move into Tim's luxury flat when he made
her an offer she couldn't refuse. If Lisa would give him
painting lessons, she could have free board in return.
She paused fractionally in the middle of a long, sen-
suous stretch, expecting to hear Tim ordering her to get
back up on the table and pose for him. Sure enough,

she heard the unmistakable sound of footsteps halting in the doorway. Lisa gave one last, voluptuous wriggle, hoisted herself on the table, flung the drapery dramatically around her and addressed him over her shoulder.

'Hurry up, sweetie. I can't wait another minute.'

'Now there's a tempting invitation,' murmured the hoarse voice of a total stranger.

Lisa froze in shock, then swung round.

'Who on earth——' she began, then flushed to the roots of her hair as she realized she had only made matters worse. Instead of a discreet partial rear view, the stranger was now getting a full frontal and enjoying every moment of it to judge by the gleam in his ice-blue eyes. Lisa had a confused impression of a tall, powerfully built man dressed in an autumn-toned checked jacket, beige slacks and a striped tie. The amused contempt in his smile galvanized her into action. She snatched at the silk drapery and tried to wind it protectively around her as she stood up. That was a fatal mistake. As she scrambled off the dining table she tripped and fell to the floor with a startled shriek, losing half her covering in the process.

'Dear me,' said the stranger softly. 'I seem to have given you a surprise.'

He crouched down as if to help her, but only succeeded in stepping on her sari.

'Don't touch me!' yelped Lisa, scrabbling vainly at the length of silk. Was he deliberately standing on it? 'Who are you? How did you get in?'

His reply came in a lazy drawl, as if this were nothing but a routine social occasion.

'My name is Matt Lansdon. I'm Tim's uncle. The door was unlocked so I just came up. I presume you must be Lisa Hayward?'

'Tim's uncle?'

Lisa stepped back a pace in shock as she realized that this was the ogre she had heard so much about, the hard-hearted trustee who had thwarted Tim's burning desire to study art and insisted that he do economics at Melbourne University instead. Subconsciously she realized that she had been expecting a white-haired, fire-breathing old dragon of about eighty, but this man was relatively young. Certainly no more than thirty-five or thirty-six, with a hard, tough, youthful physique and only a faint silvering of the temples and an indefinable aura of authority as emblems of the power he held over his nephew. As Lisa continued to gape at him, he spoke again, like a lawyer cross-examining a witness.

'I assume you must be Lisa Hayward?'

'Yes, how did you know?' she demanded defensively.

'I've heard a lot about you,' he replied.

There was a steely note in his voice, which sent a shiver of misgiving through her. For a moment he looked at her as if she was something that had crawled out from beneath a log, so that her chin came up and her eyes flashed dangerously. Then she made an effort to see things from his point of view. After all, it was hardly surprising if he disapproved of her, considering the cir-cumstances in which they had met. In a desperate at-tempt to regain her poise she wrenched the sari out from under his foot and swathed herself in it.

'I—I'm sorry about this,' she stammered. 'Tim and I were just about to...' Her voice trailed away as she realized suddenly that the painting lessons she was giving Tim were supposed to be a deadly secret. Matt Lansdon gave her a sardonic smile.

'Don't explain,' he begged. 'I can imagine what you were just about to do. You're Tim's lodger, I gather?

So tell me, what's the arrangement? Do you pay him rent and share expenses or something of that sort?'

'Yes,' agreed Lisa unhappily. 'Well, that is ... I don't exactly pay rent. We have another arrangement.'

'Indeed? How interesting. You know, you make me more and more anxious to see Tim and have a little talk to him, Miss Hayward. And perhaps you and I should have a chat, too. Although you might like to get some clothes on first?'

Lisa's cheeks burned. Little chat, indeed! There was no way she wanted to talk to him! Any fool could see what he thought was going on between her and Tim, and she didn't see why she should suffer the ordeal of stammering out a lot of incoherent explanations that wouldn't make sense. Why couldn't Tim have the courage to come right out and tell his uncle the truth? That he hated economics and wanted to study art and that Lisa was trying to help him achieve his ambition in return for having a roof over her head? And where was Tim, anyway? How long could it possibly take to go to the pub across the road?

At that moment the telephone rang. Clutching her sari protectively around her, Lisa lunged at the receiver. A muted uproar of chinking glasses, bar-room conversation and the click of billiard balls immediately assaulted her.

'Lisa?'

'Tim,' she cried gladly. 'What are you doing? You said you'd only be gone five minutes!'

Tim's voice gurgled down the line at her. Lazy, amiable and already slightly slurred.

'Don't get upset, gorgeous,' he urged. 'I ran into Barbara and some of the others at the pub and we're all going to have a counter meal and then go on to a party at Tony's place, so I guess the painting session's over for today. Oh, Tony says you can come to the party with us, if you want. I don't suppose you're interested, though, are you?'

The invitation was lukewarm and Lisa's reaction was exactly the same. She thought of the horseplay, the drinking, the numerous dogmatic arguments about the meaning of life that always seemed to go on at student parties and immediately felt as though she was approaching her hundredth birthday.

'No, thanks, Tim,' she said crisply. 'I don't feel like a party and you can't go right now, either. Your uncle Matt is here and he wants to have an urgent talk with you.'

There was a muffled groan at the other end of the line.

'Uncle Matt? Hell, I'm out of here! See you later, Lisa.'

'Tim, he wants to speak to you! You can't just hang up——'

Suddenly Matt shouldered her aside and grabbed the phone from her hands.

'Timothy? I'm warning you——'

There was a distant click at the other end of the line and Matt gave a snort of exasperation. His eyes were narrowed to mere slits of cold blue light as he put down the receiver, and the set of his mouth left Lisa in no doubt at all that he was very angry.

'Young fool!' he growled. 'When is that boy going to learn that he can't escape trouble by ducking out of a difficult situation? He hasn't even got the guts to stand by you, and I'm supposed to believe that he's mature enough to run his own life! Heaven preserve us, I think Sonia's right for once!'

Lisa stared at him with a puzzled frown. What on earth did he mean by talking about Tim standing by her? And what did Tim's mother, Sonia, have to do with it? Was Matt Lansdon unbalanced? He didn't look unbalanced! He looked like a powerful man unused to being thwarted and very annoyed about it. She forgot these speculations as Matt suddenly turned his anger on her.

'Well, Tim may have escaped for the moment,' he said in a hard voice. 'But that still leaves you, sweetheart, and you and I have a lot to discuss. I suggest you begin by getting dressed in something more substantial than a sheet of cling wrap.'

His contemptuous tone touched Lisa on the raw. After all, it wasn't her fault that Tim had hung up, leaving his uncle in the lurch, and she certainly hadn't invited Matt Lansdon to enter the house and see her naked.

'I'll get dressed when and if I choose to!' she flared. 'May I remind you, Mr Lansdon, that this is my home and you are an uninvited visitor here? What's more, I'm not your sweetheart and I don't like being spoken to in that tone of voice.'

His reply was low, silky, threatening.

'And may I remind you, Miss Hayward, that I am the legal owner of this flat? Tim is my tenant, not you, and he has no right to sublet without my permission. I could throw you out on the street at this very moment if I chose to do so.'

Lisa was taken aback, but didn't show it. The news that Matt Lansdon was the legal owner of the flat came as a complete surprise to her, but that wasn't the real crux of the problem. She was beginning to realize that she had leapt quite blithely into her rental arrangement with Tim without having any idea of the possible repercussions. At the time it had all seemed gloriously simple. Free art lessons in exchange for free board. Yet there had been several occasions since then when Lisa had wondered whether the benefits of free accommodation really made it worthwhile putting up with Tim's often juvenile behaviour. And if she now had to suffer the blazing antagonism of his uncle, as well, the whole situation would become utterly impossible.

'I see,' she said levelly. 'In that case, perhaps you would like me to pack my belongings and leave right now?'

Matt's eyes skimmed over her, not with any sensual intent, but with a piercing scrutiny she found profoundly unnerving.

'That might well be the best solution,' he rasped. 'And it's certainly what Sonia would prefer, but I want a few answers first. Before you go anywhere else, Miss Hayward, you're going to give them to me. Get dressed at once and we'll have a little chat about what's been going on here since you moved in with Tim.'

Lisa felt a sinking sensation. Tim's uncle was wearing the gloating expression of a dentist intent on performing a series of thorough and painful extractions. She wouldn't stand a chance if he started interrogating her.

'I can't!' she gabbled, improvising wildly. 'I have an appointment at the hairdresser's in fifteen minutes' time and after that I'm going to the opera at the State Theatre.'

Why had she said that? Perhaps because she would have given her eyeteeth to go to the performance of *Carmen* tonight. As usual, she couldn't possibly afford a ticket, but Matt Lansdon didn't know that. And at least it should get rid of him!

'Indeed?' drawled Matt sceptically. 'What a pity. Still, the solution's obvious. I'll go to the opera, too, and we'll have supper together afterwards. That should give us plenty of time to talk.'

Lisa flashed him a stricken look.

'Y-you can't,' she stammered.

'Why not? It's the simplest thing in the world. Oh, but you'd better give me your ticket so that I can go to the box office and arrange for you to sit with me. Have you got it somewhere handy?'

'Um...no...actually I've lost it! I was going to see if I could buy another one when I arrived there.'

'Really? Well, there's no need for that. I'll organize it all. You'll come as my guest, of course.'

She could see perfectly well that he didn't believe her, and humiliation scorched through her. Yet she wouldn't give him the satisfaction of admitting she had lied.

'How nice of you to invite me,' cooed Lisa.

The flash of angry amusement in his eyes showed that he had caught the irony in her tone. His dark eyebrows peaked.

'It's not an invitation, Miss Hayward, it's more in the nature of an order.'

'Why should I take orders from you?' she whipped back.

The cynical amusement in his expression grew more apparent than ever.

'If you have the slightest concern for Tim's welfare, you will,' he replied curtly. 'I'll pick you up at seven. Good day to you, Miss Hayward.'

Once he had left and Lisa had carefully locked the front door after him, she sank down in a dining chair, buried her head in her hands and groaned.

'What's going on here?' she demanded aloud. 'Why is he so hostile to me? I know I had no clothes on, but he surely can't think I've seduced his precious nephew!

Anyway, doesn't he know that Tim's having a torrid affair with Barbara Simpson? No, of course that's not the kind of thing that Tim would admit to good old Uncle Matt, is it? And who could blame him? Still, I could murder the stupid kid for running off and leaving me to deal with all this. Lord, what a mess! I've a good mind to go out and not be here at seven o'clock when his wretched uncle comes back.'

All the same, Matt's parting shot had been shrewdly aimed. As Lisa ran a steaming hot bubble bath and lowered herself into it with the bathroom door locked— she wasn't going to risk a second interruption—she pondered his words. What possible connection could there be between Tim's welfare and Lisa's acceptance of Matt's invitation? And hadn't there been something vaguely sarcastic in his tone, as if he didn't believe Lisa had the slightest interest in Tim's welfare? It was all very puzzling, and she had to admit that her curiosity was stirred, although there were also other, less comfortable feelings simmering inside her.

The thought of going to the opera with Matt filled her with mingled dread and annoyance. Normally she would have jumped at the chance, since she adored the drama and passion and vitality of opera but could rarely afford tickets. Yet the thought of sitting side by side in an auditorium all evening with Matt Lansdon was about as appealing as being escorted by a sabre-toothed tiger, and a hungry one at that. And that was not a bad image, she reflected, soaping a sponge and brushing it dreamily over her breasts. There was definitely something primitive and feral about the man that seemed all the more dangerous in contrast to his impeccably tailored clothing. Now that she thought about it, she remembered that Tim had told her his uncle was a grazier in Tasmania, and he certainly dressed like one. The aura of old money, old Georgian houses and antiquated notions about masculine power and importance clung to Matt Lansdon as persistently as the leathery aroma of his expensive aftershave. A deeply conservative man, if Lisa was any judge. And yet beneath the conservatism lurked something wild that sent an odd, unwelcome thrill through her.

Trying to recall every word and look and gesture that had passed between them, she found herself remembering how the dark hairs curled around the band of his Rolex watch on his left wrist, how his muscular thighs thrust against the fabric of his slacks, how his broad, powerful shoulders filled out the Fletcher Jones jacket. A faint grin curved her lips as she realized what a shock it must have given him to burst in on her and find her wearing no clothes at all. Although I suppose I'd have been shocked, too, if the situation had been reversed, admitted Lisa fairly, but that thought brought another in its train. What would Matt Lansdon look like without any clothes? He would have massive shoulders, powerful arms, a narrow waist, muscular thighs, she felt fairly sure of all that. But what about the features she hadn't seen? A hairy chest and a line of dark hair arrowing down from his navel to... Lisa blushed and slid under the water at the image that rose to her mind.

What had got into her to be thinking this sort of thing? She didn't even like the man! He was rude, arrogant and domineering, and there was no reason something should melt and flutter deep inside her at the thought of seeing him naked. She must stop having torrid, adolescent fantasies and decide what to do about his invitation. Should she go or not? It would certainly be more comfortable never to see him again. But if Tim's welfare was involved, she really had no choice about confronting his

alarming uncle. However infuriating her flatmate might
be at times, she was genuinely fond of him. Ever since
she had first met Tim, Lisa had suspected uneasily that
his family was exerting too much pressure on him and
had felt that someone ought to tackle them about it.
Well, perhaps the someone was her and this was her
opportunity.

She took special care over dressing and applying her
make-up. Not that she wanted to impress Matt Lansdon,
she told herself fiercely, but simply because she wanted
to do justice to the atmosphere of the opera itself. It
gave her a brief pang of regret that nobody seemed to
wear long dresses these days, but she chose the next best
thing. A figure-hugging jade-green sheath with a low-
cut, square neckline and a bodice embellished with in-
tricate beading and embroidery. She brushed her long,
curly dark auburn hair back from her face and fastened
it with a pearl clip that had the double advantage of
letting her display the creamy line of her throat, while
at the same time sending her curling locks rippling down
her back as she moved. A pearl choker around her neck,
gold and pearl-drop earrings with black stockings and
a gold evening bag completed the ensemble. Satisfied
with her clothes, Lisa turned her attention to her make-
up. Gazing critically at herself in the mirror, she wished
for the millionth time that her mouth wasn't so wide and
that her nose didn't have a bump in it. Well, she would
just have to attempt a little bit of camouflage! She ap-
plied a light foundation that hid her freckles, smoothed
on some gold eye shadow to bring out the highlights in
her toffee brown eyes, added some blusher high on her
cheekbones before outlining her mouth vividly with a
dark, burgundy lipstick. Then she sprayed on a liberal
cloud of Jicky Guerlain perfume and struck a pose with

one hand behind her head like a 1920s vamp. At that moment the doorbell rang. An unexpected feeling of breathlessness overtook Lisa as she ran down to answer it.

Matt Lansdon stood on the doorstep, looking grim, unsmiling and diabolically attractive. The formal black tuxedo, white shirt and black bow tie suited his rugged masculinity to perfection. His dark, wavy hair was brushed back from his forehead, his mouth was set in a tough line and his eyebrows met in a thoughtful scowl above vivid blue eyes. He did not smile at Lisa's appearance, but she thought she saw a flash of surprised approval in his eyes as he scanned her from head to foot.

'Good evening, Miss Hayward,' he said neutrally. 'Are you ready to leave?'

As he helped her on with her coat, Lisa glanced at him over her shoulder with a small, troubled smile.

'Can't you call me Lisa?' she asked. 'It seems so unfriendly to go on calling me Miss Hayward.'

His eyes narrowed into such a hostile expression that she half expected the retort that unfriendliness was exactly what he felt towards her. Instead he gave her a small, formal nod.

'Very well...Lisa,' he said stiffly. 'And I suppose you'd better call me Matt.'

She smiled at him, aware that her eyes were dancing and the dimples were showing in her cheeks.

'Thank you, Matt,' she said in a breathy, little-girl voice that she had used to charm packets of sweets out of elderly great-uncles when she was six years old.

It failed dismally with Matt. His mouth hardened and his hand tightened briefly on her elbow as if he was consciously resisting the impulse to strangle her.

'Come along,' he urged. 'We'd better not keep our driver waiting.'

As she followed him out on to the footpath, she was startled to see that there was a limousine waiting outside with a chauffeur in a grey uniform waiting respectfully to help them into the back seat. Lisa blinked.

'Are you always driven around by a chauffeur?' she marvelled, as the car glided away from the curb.

'No,' growled Matt. 'Only when I'm in Melbourne or Sydney and don't want the bother of driving myself.'

'Oh,' muttered Lisa, settling into her seat and eyeing him doubtfully. It would have been nice to think that he had planned this as a special experience for her, but even her optimistic nature couldn't accept that explanation. It was obvious that Matt Lansdon felt a powerful antagonism towards her, although she still wasn't really sure why. As the car glided along through the streets of St Kilda towards the city, she thrust that small, niggling worry out of her mind and concentrated on enjoying herself. She had always loved this hour of the day when the neon lights of the city began to sparkle like coloured jewels against the backdrop of the silvery twilight. A soft sigh of pleasure escaped her.

'I'm so glad they're performing *Carmen* tonight,' she murmured, half to herself. 'It's my favourite opera.'

'I thought it might be,' said Matt with a sardonic curl of his lips. 'The heroine seems like the kind of character who would appeal to you.'

'A gypsy slut with no heart and no morals who makes her lover suffer so cruelly that he stabs her in a jealous fit of rage? That's the kind of character you think I could identify with?'

'Yes.'

Lisa's eyes flashed dangerously.

'It must be wonderful to be able to sum up people's characters the moment you meet them without having to bother about getting to know them,' she purred. 'I'm afraid it's a skill I've never had and I might make terribly embarrassing blunders if I tried it. Take you, for instance. If I were foolish enough to go by my first impressions, I might think that you were arrogant, ill-mannered, prone to jumping to conclusions. Whereas no doubt if I wait, eventually you'll be revealed to me as gracious, fair-minded, and with a heart as soft as a marshmallow.'

Matt scowled silently at her for a moment. Then he cleared his throat.

'I'm sorry if I seem discourteous,' he muttered. 'I'll do my best to be fair-minded about whatever you have to say to me this evening.'

'Yes, why don't you do that?' agreed Lisa sweetly. 'That way I'm sure we'll both have a very pleasant evening.'

In some ways it was a very pleasant evening, although she could not remain unaware of the mysterious tension that seemed to be bubbling between them. Yet Lisa had a naturally cheerful disposition, so that even with Matt brooding silently beside her, she was still able to enjoy the magical atmosphere of the State Theatre. The women in their beautiful, shimmering dresses, the men looking splendid and formal in their dark suits, the sounds of instruments tuning up in the orchestra pit, the dim house lights, the rustle of programmes and then the colour and vitality of the stage sets and the costumes and the glorious, swirling music all combined to lift her spirits.

During the interval they did not join the rest of the throng, battling for glasses of champagne at the bar, but Matt ushered her into a private room, where the members of the opera board and their guests were mingling. To Lisa's relief, he set aside his ill humour here and escorted her around from group to group, introducing her as if she was a cherished guest. Fortunately Lisa was in her element and recognised several people she knew from art gallery openings. She was soon deep in a conversation about the stage sets for the production, which had been painted by one of her old art school cronies, so she simply smiled and nodded when Matt asked her to excuse him so he could speak to a business associate. Later as they filed into the auditorium for the second half of the opera, she found him gazing at her with a thoughtful, appraising look, as if he was surprised that she had fitted in so well with his friends.

'What's wrong?' she whispered wickedly in his ear as the house lights went down. 'Did you think I was going to rip all my clothes off and lie on the table?'

Just before the orchestra came in on cue, she could hear the audible grinding of his teeth. However, the rest of the performance was so magnificent that Lisa's thoughts were soon swept away from the mysterious subject of why Matt disliked her so much. Both of them became absorbed in the performance and, when the opera reached its stunning climax and the final curtain fell, they rose to their feet cheering and clapping with the rest of the audience. Only after half a dozen curtain calls had been taken and her hands were stinging from clapping did Lisa stop applauding and turn to look at Matt.

'Wasn't it wonderful?' she breathed. 'Thank you so much for bringing me.'

His eyes kindled.

'My pleasure,' he murmured. 'It doubles the enjoyment to be with someone who appreciates it so much.'

Yet as they went up in the lift to the restaurant up-stairs, Lisa sensed that the brief truce was over. She still felt magically uplifted and would have liked nothing better than to enjoy the discreet opulence of the res-taurant with its candelit tables and its murals of famous opera sets from the past, but she had an uneasy certainty that Matt was spoiling for a fight. All the same, her earlier shot about his manners seemed to have gone home.

'I think we should enjoy our meal and have a little chat to get to know each other better before we discuss anything really heavy, don't you?' he suggested with a wintry smile as they sat down.

'Yes, I do,' agreed Lisa candidly. 'I'm starving and I won't enjoy my food so much if you quarrel with me while I eat.'

Matt gave an explosive growl of laughter.

'Well, that's honest,' he conceded. 'And I've always liked women who enjoy food. It makes me feel they would enjoy everything else about life, as well. So tell me, my ravenous little sex goddess, what are you planning on eating?'

'Sex goddess?' challenged Lisa with a lift of her eyebrows.

'If you don't want to be considered a sex goddess, you shouldn't lie around looking so luscious on dining tables,' warned Matt in a hoarse, smoky voice, his blue eyes scanning her lazily from under half-lowered lids. 'Nor, for that matter, should you wear cocktail dresses that show off your considerable physical charms to such ad-vantage. I'll say this much for my nephew—the boy evi-dently recognises a beautiful woman when he sees one.'

Lisa stared at him uneasily. There was something in the sultry, caressing way Matt was watching her that sent an unwilling tingle of excitement through her entire body, but at the same time she resented his frank appraisal of her attractions, particularly when she was still well aware of his underlying hostility towards her. And where on earth did Tim come into this? Tim certainly didn't think she was beautiful. As a matter of fact, he often told her quite cheerfully that she ought to go on a diet. Unwilling to be drawn into a difficult discussion, Lisa simply flashed Matt a mysterious, fleeting smile and turned her attention to the menu.

'I think I'll have the seafood brochettes with wild rice and salad,' she announced. 'And perhaps the chocolate mousse cake and coffee to follow, if you don't mind. I didn't have any dinner tonight.'

'Be my guest,' Matt shrugged. 'I think I'll have the grilled lobster, myself. Would you like some champagne to drink with it?'

'Yes, please,' agreed Lisa. Once the champagne had been brought and approved, Matt leaned back in his chair and smiled at her. The smile worried Lisa. There was something dangerous about it, as if it was the opening move in a war game.

'Tell me some more about yourself,' he invited.

Lisa was just about to embark on this agreeable activity when there was a sudden interruption. A tall, flamboyant-looking man, dressed in a dinner suit of royal blue satin and with long, blond hair pulled back into a ponytail, stopped at her table and uttered a glad cry of recognition.

'Lisa! I haven't seen you for ages, darling. When are you going to give up that dreary little boyfriend of yours and come and live with me?'

Lisa gave a gurgle of laughter and returned her friend's embrace warmly. In spite of Alan's violently coloured clothes and theatrical gestures, she knew perfectly well that he was devoted to his wife, Vicky, and his two little boys. But this sort of banter was an old habit going back to their student days at art college, and she always enjoyed it.

'Whenever you say the word, sweetheart,' she replied. 'By the way, I thought your sets were magnificent tonight. Alan, have you met Matt Lansdon? Matt, this is Alan, who designed the sets for the production.'

'How do you do?' muttered Matt, rising to his feet and extending his hand.

There was a stormy glint in his eyes as he took in every detail of Alan's unconventional appearance, but the set designer seemed in no way taken aback by this scrutiny. He winked at Lisa and gave her shoulder an affectionate squeeze before he began to thread his way between the tables again.

'Well, I must be going,' he said over his shoulder. 'Nice meeting you, Matt. I envy you your supper partner. Isn't she the sexiest little moll in town?'

Matt's face was like thunder as he glared after Alan's departing back.

'Are you aware that he's a married man with two children?' he hissed when Alan was safely out of earshot.

Lisa smiled tranquilly. She found Matt's disapproval so exquisitely humorous that she couldn't bear to spoil the fun by telling him how harmless the friendship really was. Instead she gave him a long, sultry look from under lowered eyelashes and pouted at him.

'Yes,' she breathed.

For a moment she thought Matt was going to jump up out of his chair and box her ears, but instead he simply scowled at her.

'Where did you meet him?' he asked.

'Alan? We were at art school together.'

'Oh, so you really do have some claim to be a genuine artist, do you?' asked Matt in a surprised voice. 'I thought... no, never mind.'

Lisa gave him a puzzled frown and then shook her head regretfully.

'No, I don't think I can really claim to be a genuine artist,' she said flatly.

'But you just said you went to art school.'

'That doesn't make me an artist,' she retorted. 'Not by my reckoning, at any rate. I have an art school diploma and I've sold maybe a dozen reasonably important paintings over the last three years, but only at very moderate prices. I couldn't possibly live on what I earn from my art, and that's my definition of an artist. One of these days I will be a genuine artist, if hard work has anything to do with it. In the meantime I support myself in whatever way I can, but I won't claim to be something I'm not.'

Matt gazed at her thoughtfully and took a sip of his champagne.

'That's interesting,' he said, half to himself. 'You strike me as being a very ambitious young woman.'

She shrugged. 'I suppose you could say that.'

'How old are you now?' he asked.

'Twenty-five,' replied Lisa ruefully. 'So I've been at it long enough to know that it isn't easy to make a name for yourself as a painter. But one of these days I'll do it, whatever sacrifices I have to make.'

'Aren't you afraid that marriage and children will cramp your style?' asked Matt.

Since Lisa wasn't at all sure that she ever wanted to marry, that question didn't faze her.

'I have no intention of letting marriage and children cramp my style!' she replied with a toss of her head.

'I see,' said Matt grimly as he speared a piece of lobster with his fork. 'You're one of these liberated women, are you?'

There was so much distaste in his tone that Lisa had to hide a grin.

'Have I said something funny?' demanded Matt.

'No. It's more the way you said it, as if you were asking, "Oh, you're one of those poisonous snakes, are you? Or one of those deadly spiders? Or one of those white pointer sharks?"'

'Any of those would be preferable in my view to a liberated woman,' said Matt disdainfully, picking up his champagne glass again.

Lisa choked. 'You take my breath away,' she said.

'I'm astonished that any man should have the power to do that. You strike me as the sort of woman who would be glib and fluent in any situation whatsoever.'

'Thank you,' purred Lisa. 'I assume that's a compliment.'

'It isn't,' replied Matt evenly. 'But we'll let it pass for the moment. Tell me, have you known Tim long?'

There was something in the way he asked the question that made Lisa feel as if she was in a fencing ring, circling around a far more experienced, agile and deadly opponent. An odd, simmering sense of excitement began to tingle through her as she braced herself for the impending clash of swords. Then she told herself not to be melodramatic. After all, wasn't this what they had come out for? To discuss Tim's future like two calm, rational adults? She shrugged and gave Matt a faint smile.

'About six months,' she replied. 'I've been living with him for three months of that time.'

A muscle twitched in Matt's cheek at this revelation, but he continued methodically eating his lobster for a moment before glancing across at her with appraising blue eyes.

'And what do you think of him?' he demanded.

Lisa hesitated. There was a lot she wanted to say, but Tim had strictly forbidden her to say most of it. He was morbidly afraid of the sort of angry scene he believed would ensue if his mother and uncle discovered that he was still pursuing his passion for art against their wishes. Left to herself, Lisa would have been perfectly frank with Matt. She would have told him that his nephew showed extraordinary promise as a painter and begged him to let the youth give up his half-hearted study of economics and go to art school full time. Yet Tim had sworn her to secrecy and she did not feel that she could betray his trust. Her misgivings showed in her face.

'There's no need to be tactful,' urged Matt irritably. 'I want the truth from you. What are your impressions of my nephew's character?'

Tim's character! Well, it was easier to be truthful about that than about his ambitions. Tim had never sworn her to secrecy about his character.

'He's basically a nice boy,' she replied in the measured tone of a headmistress giving a character reference. 'Although he is rather spoilt and he seems to think he can have whatever he wants simply by demanding it.'

'That's Sonia's influence,' said Matt in an exasperated voice. 'She's a very silly woman and she gave in to him too much when he was a child. Still, I suppose it's not surprising that she spoiled the boy after his father died.'

'How did his father die?' asked Lisa hesitantly. 'Tim has never told me.'

A shadow crossed Matt's features.

'He was piloting a light aircraft, which crashed. Tim was only two years old at the time.'

Something in the grim lines of Matt's face told her that long-ago grief still haunted him. She thought about how she would feel if her own adored brother, Brian, had met with such a disaster and instinctively flinched.

'I suppose he was your older brother, wasn't he?' she said huskily. 'I'm so sorry.'

Matt's gaze darted swiftly across the table to meet hers, as if he was startled by the sympathy in her voice. Then he shrugged.

'Thank you,' he replied. 'But it was a long time ago. I seldom think of it now.'

'You can't have been very old when it happened.'

'I was eighteen. There was a ten-year age gap between my brother and myself.'

'Only eighteen?' she exclaimed. 'And yet he made you trustee for the whole estate?'

Matt's mouth hardened. 'Yes. He thought I was the tough one in the family and he knew I was shrewd at handling money even then. I bought my first portfolio of shares when I was sixteen. You'd do well to remember that, Lisa.'

Lisa gave him a baffled look. Why would she do well to remember it? What did it have to do with her? Although perhaps this was the opening she had been waiting for, to turn the conversation round to Tim's interests again. If she could persuade Matt to give Tim more financial freedom, perhaps she need not even mention the delicate subject of art.

'Can I ask you something?' she said. 'If you wanted to, could you wind up the trust and leave Tim in control of his money?'

'Yes,' said Matt in a clipped tone.

Lisa let out a long sigh.

'I really think you ought to do that,' she urged.

'Why should I?' demanded Matt suspiciously. 'He'll come into his inheritance at the age of twenty-five in any case, and all his expenses are paid for him at the moment. He doesn't go short of anything.'

'No, he doesn't go short of anything,' agreed Lisa passionately. 'But he doesn't have control of anything, either, and that really infuriates him. I'm sure he wouldn't get involved in so many silly stunts at the university if he didn't feel so hemmed in by you and his mother. In my opinion, half the reason he's so silly and disruptive is that he feels as if he's treated like a child.'

'Does he now?' said Matt dryly. 'Well, he'll simply have to put up with it until I'm convinced that it's in his best interests to change my approach. And I'm not convinced of that yet. Tell me, are you in love with Tim?'

Lisa choked with laughter.

'Of course not!' she retorted.

'Yet you live with him?' demanded Matt sternly.

All the hostility between them seemed to come bubbling to the surface as the implication of his words sank in.

'So you assume——' cried Lisa hotly and then bit off the words.

'I've seen for myself that you lie around naked on the dining table inviting his attentions,' continued Matt in a hushed, rapid tone so that she had to strain her ears to catch the words. 'So I assume that you're having an affair with him. Is that unreasonable?'

Lisa flushed scarlet and glanced uneasily around her, but the other guests in the restaurant seemed quite unconscious of what they were discussing. Her mind raced as she tried to gather her thoughts. She could have told Matt Lansdon the simple truth, every bit of it, including the bargain about the art lessons. But why should she? What business was it of his?

'It's nothing to do with you,' she flared.

'I see,' he replied mockingly. 'Then I'll simply have to go on making my assumptions, won't I? But if you're not in love with Tim, are you at least fond of him?'

'As a matter of fact, I am!'

'Then leave him alone, Lisa,' urged Matt, leaning forward across the table and seizing her wrist. 'Move out of that flat and give him a chance to grow up. He doesn't need a woman like you in his life when he's barely out of school and still wet behind the ears.'

'A woman like me?' echoed Lisa. 'And what exactly is that supposed to mean?'

'You know damned well what it's supposed to mean. You're a sensual, ambitious little schemer and you're using your considerable charm and physical attraction to lure him into your nets.'

'I'm flattered that you think I have charm and physical attraction,' jeered Lisa.

'Don't be. It's a simple statement of fact, not a compliment. What baffles me is why you bother. Is the money really worth it?'

'What money?' demanded Lisa contemptuously.

'The money you hope to get when Tim marries you,' snapped Matt.

Lisa's mouth fell open. 'Is *that* what I'm supposed to be after? Marriage to Tim?'

'Oh, I love the bewildered innocence, sweetheart! But you're wasting your time trying to fool me. Sonia's already told me you and Tim are planning to get married.'

Lisa very nearly picked up the champagne bottle and emptied it over Matt's head. Then she took a long, deep breath and exhaled slowly. She had disliked Tim's mother from the moment she met her, considering her snobbish, patronizing and extremely silly, but even Sonia was incapable of such a pearl of fantasy without at least a grain of truth to get her started. Tim must have said something to set this whole tale in motion!

'Where did you hear this?' she asked.

'Tim told her. She says she's found you in the house twice when she went to visit him. The first time she suspected you were living with him, so the second time she arrived unannounced, found a wild party in progress and Tim draped all over you.'

'It wasn't a wild party!' protested Lisa. 'It was just a few of Tim's friends at the end of third term. We've had much wilder parties than that.'

'Have you?' demanded Matt in an ominous tone. 'As your landlord, I hardly find that reassuring. Anyway, be that as it may, Sonia tackled Tim about it afterwards and demanded to know what you were doing there. At first he told her a lot of implausible stories and then finally blurted out the truth—that he had fallen in love with you and was planning to marry you.'

Lisa gave a low gasp of indignation.

'That idiot,' she muttered. 'I might have known he'd go to pieces once Sonia started interrogating him. He's nothing but a big, silly kid.'

'Exactly,' growled Matt. 'So why are you wasting your time on him? You don't need a boy, you need a grown man, and a powerful one at that, to keep you occupied, young lady.'

'Oh, so you're offering your services, are you?' demanded Lisa sarcastically.

Matt's hold on her wrist tightened.

'I might be, I just might be,' he growled. 'Not marriage, Lisa. I've no intention of marrying a woman who's available to the highest bidder, but a love affair, that's something else.' He leaned forward and his voice was so low that she could scarcely catch the words, but when she did they made her quiver with rage and something else. 'I can make you tingle and ache with sexual passion in a way that boy hasn't even discovered yet. You're a gambler and a deeply sensual woman, Lisa, and I'm a man of considerable experience. Why don't you try your luck with me?'

CHAPTER TWO

LISA was so outraged by this question that for a moment she was completely speechless. Yet if she was honest, it was not only outrage that she felt. A strange, throbbing warmth began to pulsate deep inside her at Matt's words, and the intense, stormy look in his eyes made her feel breathless. Feeling almost as angry with herself as with him, she jerked her hand out of his grip and gave him a cold, challenging stare.

'What exactly are you suggesting?' she demanded.

Matt smiled lazily as if he was enjoying the situation.

'I'm a wealthy man,' he said in a low voice. 'I could set you up in style with a luxury flat and a studio. I already come to Melbourne quite frequently on business and I could come even more frequently for pleasure.'

Lisa felt the taste of rage in her mouth, as pure and toxic as neat alcohol.

'You make me sound like a fast food outlet,' she hissed. 'Juicy steaks, medium rare, prepared to perfection while you wait! And our money back guarantee if we fail to satisfy.'

Matt looked at her from under half-closed lids.

'Oh, I don't think you'd fail to satisfy,' he murmured.

She leapt to her feet with an inarticulate gasp of rage.

'I've never been so insulted in my life!' she cried.

Matt seized her wrist again. Gently, tenderly, as if this was nothing more than a playful disagreement between them. Yet there was something merciless in that grip.

'Sit down,' he invited. 'I haven't finished with you.'

'Well, I've finished with you!' she flared and turned as if to flee.

His grip tightened. There was a latent physical force in that warm, hard, masculine hand that enthralled and alarmed her. He wasn't actually hurting her, she couldn't say that, but he was making her aware in the most blatant possible way of his virility and strength. With a sense of disbelief, she realized that the only way she could escape would be to shout for help and knock over a few wineglasses. For one wild moment she seriously contemplated the prospect. But Matt's wordless, lingering smile made her decide against it. He might seem conservative on the surface, but with a sudden flash of insight she guessed that he was really totally indifferent to the opinion of others. If she made a scene, he was probably perfectly capable of swinging her over his shoulder and marching out of the restaurant. Shuddering inwardly at the image, Lisa subsided into her seat and glared at him.

'Am I to take it that your answer is no?' he asked mildly.

'Yes,' said Lisa between her teeth.

'Your answer is yes?' marvelled Matt, deliberately misunderstanding her. 'What an unexpected pleasure! I'm sure we'll get along brilliantly together.'

'I didn't mean that!' flared Lisa, losing all patience. 'I meant yes, my answer is no. Oh, stop trying to make me sound stupid! I wouldn't have an affair with you if you were the last man on earth.'

'And yet you're prepared to do it with Tim?' he challenged.

'Well, he says he's going to marry me, doesn't he?' demanded Lisa sarcastically. 'He told Sonia so, didn't he? I'd hardly be likely to give up the prospect of marrying Tim just so that I could go to bed with you, now would I?'

'You'd be wiser if you did,' growled Matt, dropping his benevolent pose. 'A marriage between you and Tim would never work.'

'Why not?' asked Lisa angrily.

'He's not up to your weight,' retorted Matt.

'If you're going to make cheap shots about my figure——' began Lisa.

'I'm not talking about your figure!' cut in Matt impatiently. 'It's magnificent, as you well know. I'm talking about your personality, your style. I've seen enough of you to know that you have vitality, gusto, humour and blatant sex appeal. Compared to you, Tim is nothing but a colourless boy. Maybe in a few years he'll gain some colour, but not if he's stuck in your shadow. Lisa, I'm appealing to your better nature. Give him up!'

Lisa scowled at him. She was secretly flattered by his comments about her vitality and sex appeal and she couldn't help agreeing with his assessment of Tim. All the same, she felt it was underhanded of Matt to try to appeal to her better nature after he had already leapt to such outrageous conclusions about her greed and ruthlessness. She still felt angry and offended and wanted to go on fighting with him until she had evened the score before she laid down her weapons.

'What makes you think I have a better nature?' she cooed.

Matt's eyes flashed ominously.

'Then you won't give him up?' he challenged.

Lisa smiled provocatively, enjoying the heady sensation of power that his uneasiness was giving her.

'Tell me one good reason why I should.'

'Money.'

'What?'

Lisa almost fell off her chair.

'I thought that would make you take notice,' said Matt contemptuously. 'All right, here's the deal. I'll pay you if you promise to move out of Tim's flat and stay away from him for a year.'

Lisa stared at her companion in disbelief. Was it a joke? No, it couldn't possibly be. Matt's expression was grimly serious and he was already reaching inside the pocket of his dinner jacket for a chequebook and a gold pen.

'What's to stop me from taking the money and going back on my word?' she demanded, turning over the possibilities as if it was some kind of quiz game. 'Or do you have too high an opinion of my character for that?'

'No, I don't,' retorted Matt rudely. 'Naturally I'll take precautions. The payment will be in quarterly instalments with the first one being made now as a gesture of good faith. Once you've moved out of the flat there will be three more instalments at intervals of three months, provided you keep your side of the bargain. And, believe me, I have ways of checking.'

'You mean you'll have a private detective spying on me?' she demanded.

Matt shrugged and smiled unpleasantly. Lisa let out a low gasp of rage.

'Just as a matter of interest, how much are you offering me to do this?' she demanded.

He named a figure that made her jaw drop.

'B-but that's a fortune,' she stammered.

'I take it we have an agreement then,' he said coldly, scrawling on the cheque and signing it with a flourish. 'There you are, Lisa. It's been most interesting doing business with you. Now what about my other offer of changing your allegiance from Tim to me? Are you sure you don't want to accept that, too?'

For a moment she was speechless with indignation, then belatedly she found her voice and her power of movement. With shaking fingers she snatched the cheque from Matt's hand and glanced down at it. A long row of noughts at the end blurred before her gaze. Then holding the paper as distastefully as if it were a spider, she thrust it into the candle flame.

'I have only one thing to say to you,' she told him as the acrid smoke coiled up. 'If I ever choose to marry Tim, there is no way on earth that you'll be able to stop me!'

A warning heat scorched her fingers so that she dropped the charred remnants of the cheque in the ashtray. Then, snatching her evening bag off the table, she strode to the door with her head held high and her eyes flashing. A brief pause to claim her coat and she was on her way. She was dimly aware of a hubbub behind her as a waiter bustled over to investigate the smell of smoke and Matt placated him with a substantial tip before hurrying after her. He caught up with her just as the doors of the lift were closing. Thrusting one muscular, black-clad leg between them, he forced them open and rejoined her. He looked as impeccable as ever, but something wild and dangerous lurked at the back of his ice-blue eyes. Lisa felt an irrational surge of panic as the doors closed behind him, leaving them alone together. Her heart began to thud frantically and her breath came in shallow flutters as the lift plunged downwards.

'Don't ever behave like that in public again,' he warned.

Then he swept her into his arms and kissed her. It was not just the motion of the lift that gave her that dizzy, plunging sensation. As she hurtled down the lift shaft, locked in his arms, Lisa had a giddy feeling of being totally powerless. A warning bell sounded as they reached the car park, but Matt simply reached out and pressed the button for the top floor again. He was still kissing her passionately when the door opened near the restaurant and Lisa came to her senses enough to realize where they were.

Flushing, she broke away from Matt and had to endure the disapproving glances of two elderly women and the sly grins of their spouses on their way down again. She was relieved when they parted company with the older couples and emerged into the car park, but even then her troubles were not over. Matt took her arm tranquilly and guided her towards the limousine, visible behind one of the pillars.

'I don't need a ride,' she said. 'I'm going back upstairs to call a taxi.'

'Do as you're told, Lisa,' he ordered amiably. 'I don't want to have to carry you to the car. Of course, once we're inside it you're welcome to quarrel with me, provided you don't mind William overhearing every word.'

She cast him a smouldering look.

'You brute! I hate you! How dare you maul me like that in the lift?'

Matt's voice was full of lazy amusement as he pulled her out of the path of a departing Rolls and waved cheerfully at the two older couples inside the vehicle.

'Maul you, sweetheart? What rubbish! You enjoyed every moment of it as much as I did.'

This was so close to the truth that Lisa sat fuming in silence half the way home. Her response to Matt Lansdon appalled her, but when she had finally stopped berating herself, she began to worry about the more important issue of what she should do. Well, there was really only one answer to that. Tim must be made to tell the truth and both male Lansdons must grovel apologetically at her feet. After that she would have to move out and find herself somewhere else to live. Her pride could not possibly permit her to remain in her present situation, although the prospect of finding lodgings she could afford made her spirits sink. She would have to find a waitressing job again and that would leave even less time available for painting. Besides, in spite of Tim's out-rageous behaviour, she had a niggling suspicion that she was going to miss him if she never saw him again. Of course she wouldn't miss Matt Lansdon and she hoped devoutly that she would never have to see *him* again. If only she could get through the rest of this evening, with luck she might never have to set eyes on him in future!

When they entered the flat, Lisa waved hopefully at the huge, open-plan living room, which dominated the lower floor.

'Would you like to sit down and fix yourself a drink,' she asked, 'while I go upstairs and see if Tim's home?'

'No, thanks,' replied Matt coolly. 'I'll come up and see for myself. I am one of the family, after all.'

She couldn't help resenting this invasion of the more private part of the flat, nor did it make her task any easier. If Tim had drunk too much at a party, which had happened several times lately, there would be little chance of concealing the fact from his uncle. Oh, well, perhaps it would do him good to be accountable for his actions for once! A thin rectangle of golden light under his bedroom door showed that he was at home.

'Perhaps you'd like to sit down,' invited Lisa. 'And I'll ask Tim to come out and speak to you.'

'All right,' agreed Matt.

She waited until he had taken his seat in the small sunroom off the dining area and was on the point of tapping on Tim's door when she realized that was out of character with her role as his fiancée. Instead she boldly opened the door as if it belonged to her own bedroom, slipped inside and shut it behind her. Tim was busy getting undressed and looked up with an expression of mild surprise as he pulled on a pair of navy blue silk pyjama bottoms. His upper half was still bare, but Lisa spared him no more than a glance. Tim was like a brother to her and in any case his thin, boyish physique awoke no dangerous longings in her of the kind inspired by his uncle. He pushed a lock of his silky, honey-gold hair out of his brown eyes and flashed her a mischievous grin.

'Did you get rid of Uncle Matt?' he demanded without any preliminary greeting.

'No,' said Lisa flatly, leaning back against the door. 'He's in the sunroom, waiting to talk to you.'

An expression of comic dismay flitted over Tim's features and he looked wildly around for an escape route. His gaze lingered momentarily on the curtained picture windows.

'Oh, no, you don't!' cried Lisa, darting towards him. 'There will be no ladders of knotted sheets, no death-defying human fly exits. You're going to face the music, laddie. Dear old uncle Mathew wants some answers and so do I!'

'What do you mean?' asked Tim uneasily, backing away from her.

'I'm talking about your marriage plans,' replied Lisa sweetly. 'It would have been nice if you had proposed to me before you told your mother that we were getting married.'

Tim sucked in breath with an anguished expression like a child who has just fallen on his face and grazed his hands and knees.

'Sorry,' he muttered placatingly. 'But I was in a tight corner, Lisa, and I had to say something. You know my mother. She was suspicious that first time she came round here and found you at the flat late at night, and it was even worse on her second visit. You know how she arrived at the party and we didn't even hear her let herself in? Well, she went snooping around in my bathroom and found a packet of condoms in the cupboard and Barbara's tights hanging up to dry in the shower recess. After that, she went down and cross-examined the porter and found out that I had a young woman living here. Of course, when she burst into the party and I was standing with my arm around you, she naturally jumped to the conclusion that it was you, so then she dragged me off into the study and started working herself into a state about it. I could see she was all ready to go out and embarrass me in front of my friends by having shrieking hysterics about how Mummy's boy had fallen into the clutches of a bold, bad, wicked streetwalker. I had to think up some kind of story to stop her.'

'So you told her you were in love with me and that you were going to marry me?' demanded Lisa incredulously.

'Yeah, that's about the size of it, although I didn't really think she'd be silly enough to swallow it.'

'Well, she has,' fumed Lisa. 'And what's worse, she's managed to convince your Uncle Matt, as well. That's why he's here in Melbourne. He's come to rescue you from me.'

Tim gave a muffled snort of laughter.

'It's not funny!' cried Lisa furiously. 'He actually offered me money to leave you alone.'

Tim's mirth gave way to a speculative look.

'How much did he offer you?' he asked slyly. 'Perhaps we could split the difference. I'm a bit short of funds right now.'

'You!' gasped Lisa. 'I hope you're joking, Tim. Because if you're not, that's the most unscrupulous suggestion I've ever heard. Anyway, we can't split the bribe. I've already burnt the cheque.'

'Burnt it!' echoed Tim reproachfully. 'Lisa, you've got no common sense, no prudence, no thought for the future. All those things my relatives are always telling me. You're worse than I am.'

'No, I'm not! I've got years of scheming and lying and double-dealing ahead of me before I'll be in your class, you little toad. Don't you realize you've made me look like a fool and a tart in front of your uncle?'

'Oh, come on,' protested Tim. 'Just because you're staying here in the flat? There's nothing very wicked or surprising about that! Lots of students share digs.'

'You seem to have forgotten that I was posing nude when Matt arrived,' said Lisa coldly.

Tim gave another smothered yelp of laughter. 'You mean he caught you starkers?' he cried. 'What a joke!'

'No, it wasn't! It was extremely embarrassing.'

'Oh, don't talk garbage! Matt might look as grim as a high court judge, but he's had a pretty wild sex life himself. Women fall all over themselves trying to catch him.'

'I'm not interested in Matt's sex life,' announced Lisa haughtily and quite untruthfully. 'What I'm interested in is having my good name cleared.'

'Oh, you're making a fuss about nothing. This'll soon blow over.'

'Yes, it will,' agreed Lisa. 'Provided you go out there right now and tell him the truth.'

'Are you crazy? Matt would murder me!'

'It serves you right if he does.'

'Oh, come on, Lisa, have a heart,' wheedled Tim. 'Blackening a lady's reputation, lying, cheating, preferring painting to Accountancy 101, those are all capital crimes in Uncle Matt's book. I'll never come out of that room alive if I tell him the truth.'

With a dismissive shrug he began picking up his pyjama jacket and turning down the bed, as if he had no other thought but to turn out the light and go to sleep. Lisa snatched the jacket away from him and held it behind her back.

'You wimp! You wussy! You pathetic little worm!' she accused. 'You're afraid of him, aren't you?'

'Yes,' admitted Tim candidly, making a wild snatch at the pyjama jacket.

'Well, I'm not!' cried Lisa. 'And if you don't tell him the truth, I will!'

'Why didn't you tell him already then?'

'Because I felt sorry for you, you despicable little wretch!' she replied hotly. 'Heaven knows why! And I thought it should come from you. You'd have much more chance of getting him to approve your art studies if you stood up for yourself and told him the truth. But if you're too chicken-hearted, I'll have to do it.'

A sly look began to glint in Tim's brown eyes, sending chills of misgiving up Lisa's spine.

'Wait a minute, Lisa,' he begged. 'There's something else you haven't considered.'

'What?'

'I've entered for the Buller Art Prize and the results of the competition won't be out for another six weeks. Look, I know I don't have a hope in hell of winning, but suppose a miracle happened? Three years in Paris studying art with a studio apartment and a living allowance! If I won that, Matt would have to take my painting seriously. He'd have to let me go. Or if he wouldn't, stuff it, I'd just go anyway. Can't you wait until the competition results come out before you spill the beans to him?'

'This is crazy,' faltered Lisa. 'I know you're talented, Tim, but every young artist in Australia is after that prize. It's true that your uncle would have to take you seriously if you won, but, well . . .'

Tim saw her hesitation and pounced.

'Just wait another six weeks, that's all I ask.'

'No, I won't! Your uncle has already told me I'm scheming and ambitious and I'm sick of being made to look a fool.'

'Well, get your own back on him,' urged Tim craftily. 'Make him look a fool instead. Pretend you're going to marry me and let him sweat it out for another six weeks.'

Lisa hesitated and a sly grin began to curve the edges of her mouth. The plan did have a certain evil charm. And how satisfying it would be to make that smug, disapproving Matt Lansdon as uneasy as he had made her!

'What would we tell him about us once the six weeks were up?' she objected.

Tim shrugged.

'We could always say we'd had a fight and split up,' he replied airily. 'At least it would give you time to find somewhere else to live, if that's what you want to do.'

'Well——' began Lisa uncertainly.

'I knew I could count on you, sweetie!' exclaimed Tim, sweeping her into his arms and giving her a brotherly hug. 'Let's go in and tell Uncle Matt we're thinking of an April wedding. I'll just put my pyjama top on.'

Lisa's smile broadened.

'Leave it off,' she advised.

Matt was lounging back in the leather couch with a tumbler of whisky in his hand when they entered the sunroom. Lisa felt a spurt of annoyance at the way he had made himself at home and then realized belatedly that he had every right to do so. After all, he was the owner of this flat. At the sight of them, he set down his glass and rose to his feet before stretching out his hand to his nephew.

'Tim,' he said pleasantly, but with an ominous undertone in his voice.

Tim flinched at that crushing grip, but smiled gamely.

'Hello, Uncle Matt,' he said with only a hint of nervousness beneath the bravado. 'I believe you've come to congratulate me on my engagement.'

Matt's eyebrows rose.

'So matters have gone that far, have they?' he enquired. 'Aren't you rushing things a bit?'

Tim looked as if his nerve might be about to desert him, so Lisa came to his rescue.

'Oh, no,' she sighed rapturously. 'I'm sure you know what it's like when you're in love, Matt. We just can't wait any longer to make it official.'

Matt's blue eyes flashed sparks.

'Is that so?' he murmured. 'Well, if Tim's going to support a wife, I suppose he'd better come home and get some practical experience on the farm. It will all belong to him one of these days and he's been a bit remiss about his duties so far. All that will have to change now.

I'm sure that getting up at dawn mustering sheep and mending fences will do wonders for you, lad.'

Tim gave a sickly smile. His idea of an early morning was getting up before noon and having several cups of espresso coffee in a Lygon Street cafe with Barbara.

'That's nice of you, Uncle,' he said in a failing voice. 'But I'll be busy here in Melbourne.'

'What with?' asked Matt. 'Exams are over, aren't they? What other plans do you have for the long vacation?'

Tim darted Lisa a harried glance.

'Oh, extra swotting for next year,' he said, inventing hastily. 'Or perhaps a holiday job at the Australian Stock Exchange or the Bureau of Statistics. And I really ought to get some coaching on my weak points in accountancy.'

'It's good to see you taking an interest in your studies at last,' murmured Matt with a grim smile. 'But you can do most of that back on the farm. Not the part-time jobs, of course, but certainly the coaching in accountancy. I can help you myself. We can spend all day in the saddle and the evening studying the stock market right through till midnight, if you like. Yes, yes. That's an excellent idea.'

An appalled expression crossed Tim's face.

'I—I can't!' he stammered, glancing wildly around for inspiration. 'I'd miss Lisa too much.'

Matt smiled. A hard, dangerous smile.

'Oh, Lisa must come, too,' he said in a silky voice. 'If she's going to be a farmer's wife, she's going to need to learn all the skills of running the place. Churning butter, driving tractors, cooking for the workers, dealing with snakes. I'm sure she'll have a wonderful time. And of course it will give her a chance to meet the rest of the family, too, since they're all coming for Christmas. No doubt you'll want to cook Christmas dinner for us, Lisa? It will only be a small gathering of the clan this year, no more than fifteen or twenty, I'd say. And it will give you an excellent chance to get to know Tim's mother better.'

Lisa emitted a soft wail like the sound of a whoopee cushion.

'Did you say something?' asked Matt. 'Or am I imagining things? I'm afraid I am getting rather hard of hearing. It's a hazard that afflicts elderly uncles.'

His eyes met hers, bright, hard, challenging and far from elderly. She could have given in immediately, could have told him the truth or simply refused his invitation and quietly moved out of the flat the following day. Yet Lisa was naturally obstinate. She might refuse an invitation, but never a challenge. A martial glint came into her eye and she lifted her chin defiantly.

'Thank you, Matt,' she replied. 'I'm sure Tim and I will have a lovely time staying with you.'

If Matt was disconcerted by her response he didn't show it.

'Good. I'll book the airline tickets and be back tomorrow morning to pick you up,' he promised.

Matt didn't give her a chance to renege on her agreement. He returned just as he had threatened the following morning. Tim and Lisa had risen at what they both regarded as the outrageously early hour of nine o'clock and were sharing breakfast in a decidedly unloverlike atmosphere when they heard Matt ring the front doorbell below. Lisa was having dire thoughts about the wisdom of the whole escapade and Tim was scowling moodily about the prospect of leaving Barbara and the night-life of Melbourne. The sound of the doorbell breaking in on their quarrelsome consumption of cornflakes almost came as a relief. Lisa turned red and then white and half rose to her feet at the sound.

'We ought to tell him the truth,' she said in a tormented voice.

'Don't be stupid,' protested Tim. 'He'll probably evict you on the spot and cut my allowance for the next six months if we do. Just stay cool, Lisa, and let me handle this.'

That was more easily said than done as Lisa discovered when Tim vanished downstairs and returned with his uncle in tow. Matt was just as impeccably dressed as on the previous day and radiated the same air of ruthless confidence. The fickle spring sunshine of the previous day had given way to showers and he was wearing a charcoal grey suit with a white shirt and striped tie beneath a camel-coloured cashmere overcoat. His face had the alert, dangerous look of a corporate raider engaged in a tricky takeover bid. When his eyes met Lisa's, she stared defiantly back, suddenly conscious of the thoughts that must be running through his mind as he took in every detail of her faded Levi's, figure-hugging ribbed sweater, patchwork velvet jacket and scuffed Italian hiking boots. She hadn't deliberately dressed that way in order to antagonize him, but she felt a spurt of amusement at the unmistakable flash of disapproval in his eyes. It would do him good to realize that not everybody in the world was as conservative and hidebound as him! Seeing him now, she found it impossible to believe that this stern, disapproving stranger had kissed her so violently the previous night and that she had responded with such fervour. She didn't even like him! He was arrogant, humourless and entirely too self-satisfied. He deserved to have this deception played on him!

'Well, are you both ready to go to the airport?' he asked.

'I suppose so,' muttered Tim, rising to his feet and slouching towards the door. 'Although I'd really rather stay here.'

'What about the cereal bowls?' demanded Matt.

'What about them?' retorted Tim blankly, pausing in the doorway.

'There's an old Australian custom that you two have probably never encountered,' said Matt in a hard voice. 'It's called washing up.'

Lisa smothered a grin as Tim, obedient to that hypnotic blue stare, meekly carried the two bowls into the kitchen and washed them. It had always driven her crazy the way her young flatmate blithely scattered dirty plates and dirty clothes on every available surface for her to clean up. Perhaps Matt Lansdon had his uses after all!

Ten minutes later they were all safely installed in the limousine once more, with their luggage in the boot. Matt frowned at an expensive, leather-clad diary and tapped his lower teeth with his thumbnail.

'I'm afraid I'll have to make two stops on the way to the airport,' he announced. 'I need to see my real estate agent briefly about a commercial warehouse that I'm hoping to lease. And I also have to call in to my solicitor's office to sign some documents at ten-thirty. But I won't hold you up for too long.'

The mid-morning traffic was relatively light and they made good time from St Kilda into the centre of the city, but when they reached the real estate agent's office, they suffered an unexpected setback. Tim, who had been sent inside to enquire about the lease agreement for his uncle, came back shaking his head.

'Sorry, Uncle Matt. He said it wasn't ready yet. He's expecting it by courier any time now.'

Matt gave a faint sigh of exasperation.

'Damn,' he said irritably. 'I've got some important documents to sign at Lewis, Evans and Price at ten-thirty, so I can't wait around here. I'll tell you what, Tim, you stay here and collect the package for me, will you? Take a taxi to the airport when you're ready.'

It was all done so naturally that not the slightest suspicion crossed Lisa's mind. Of course, it did make her feel uncomfortable and oddly elated to find herself alone with Matt, but since he merely stared out the window with an abstracted expression as they skimmed along the freeway, that sensation soon passed. It was not until they were waiting in the departure lounge at Tullamarine airport and their flight began boarding that she guessed anything was really wrong.

'What about Tim?' she demanded in a voice full of misgiving, as Matt took her arm and guided her into the huge, concertina-like tube that funnelled passengers into the plane. 'He hasn't arrived yet. Aren't we going to wait for him?'

'Oh, there's no need to do that,' replied Matt calmly. 'He's still got a few minutes yet, and he'll probably manage to catch the flight by the skin of his teeth. If he doesn't, he'll just have to take the afternoon plane.'

Something in his voice, some undertone of triumph alerted her. As they shuffled into the plane's interior, suspicion flowered into certainty. Lisa couldn't just stand blocking the aisle, so she sank down into one of the comfortable blue velvet seats in the first-class section, but there was a look of incredulous outrage on her face.

'You planned this, didn't you?' she demanded bitterly. 'Tell me the truth, Matt. Did you deliberately lure Tim away just so that you could keep us apart?'

CHAPTER THREE

'DON'T be silly,' said Matt with an expression of such incredulous amusement that Lisa immediately felt like a particularly gullible six-year-old. 'You heard what I said to Tim. I told him to join us at the airport. It's not the first time he's missed a plane in his life and it won't be the last. Either the documents I wanted weren't ready and he stayed to wait for them or he just couldn't get a taxi in time. There's no need to think up melodramatic explanations of why he isn't with us at this very moment. You can't seriously believe that I enticed him away or that he deliberately skipped off and left you?'

Lisa stared into those mocking blue eyes with a troubled expression. Skipped off... The words echoed in her head and she almost groaned aloud. Wasn't that an even more likely explanation than the idea that Matt had deliberately engineered all this? What if Tim had just seen his opportunity to escape from a troublesome situation and simply run for his life? Or had Matt plotted all this? Something in the fugitive smile that flickered around the edges of his mouth made her deeply uneasy. Well, if he had planned it all there was no reason she should just sit here and meekly cooperate! She was a free agent, wasn't she? She would just get up and leave!

Even as the thought crossed her mind she realized that her bags containing her best clothes and art equipment were already in the cargo hold of the aircraft and that it would seem very eccentric to jump up and leave the plane right now. The hostesses were already moving along

the aisle, slamming the overhead lockers in readiness for
its departure. Oh, who cared about seeming eccentric
anyway? If she was going to make a break, it would have
to be now or never. But was she simply making a fool
of herself? Would Tim genuinely arrive on the next plane
and wonder what had become of her? She hesitated a
fraction too long. While she was still frozen with her
hand on her seat buckle, the door that offered the only
exit from the plane was suddenly closed by a steward.
A feeling of panic and claustrophobia overtook her and
she caught her breath.

'What's wrong?' asked Matt in a concerned voice. 'Are
you afraid of flying?'

'No.' She bit back the words, 'I'm afraid of you'. Instead she said huskily, 'I'm afraid Tim might miss the
next flight, too.'

'Or not come at all?' mused Matt. 'Oh, come now,
Lisa. In ordinary circumstances I might share your misgivings. It's true that I've just paid Tim's allowance for
the long vacation into his credit account, and he does
usually like to go off on rowdy holidays with his friends
during the summer. It's no secret that he finds the family
farm dead boring. But with his future wife staying there?
Surely not! I can't believe he'll desert you if he's genuinely in love with you. And even if he does, I'm sure I
can keep you adequately entertained.'

She gazed at him in horror as the diabolical cunning
of the scheme became apparent to her. If Matt had deliberately planned this, she was going to be stranded
alone on a farm in Tasmania with him. The realization
made her so furious that she could gladly have slapped
the smile off his face. For a moment she struggled with
her feelings, then her natural sense of fairness reasserted
itself. She couldn't be sure that Matt had planned it, but

even if he had, was his behaviour really any worse than
her own? The only thing she could honestly accuse him
of was outmanoeuvring her in this war of nerves. If anything, her behaviour was probably even worse than his.
Not only had she told Matt a lot of barefaced lies, but
something occurred to her now that she had not even
considered the previous evening. She had let him pay for
her flight to Tasmania. A twinge of guilt went through
her at the realization. The whole joke was getting out
of hand....

'I want you to know that I'll pay you back for my
airline ticket,' she blurted out.

Matt looked at her with a puzzled frown.

'What on earth for?' he asked indifferently. 'You're
practically a member of the family now and I did invite
you as my guest. I wouldn't hear of your paying me
back.'

That made Lisa feel worse than ever. Here she was
branded as a slut and a schemer and she couldn't even
have the comfort of financial independence! As the plane
began to back away from the landing bay, she bit her
lip and stared out at the shiny tarmac, half obscured by
blurring rain. It only made matters worse to realize that
her own behaviour was largely responsible for Matt's
poor opinion of her. Admittedly it was sheer bad luck
that they had got off to a bad start. The fact that she
had been cavorting around the flat without a stitch of
clothing had certainly made matters awkward between
them. Yet if she had told him the truth immediately,
perhaps the awkwardness could have been smoothed
over. Instead Matt had jumped to conclusions and she
had lost her temper and told him a pack of lies.

Now the damage was done, he would probably never
believe the truth about her. That, in spite of dressing

unconventionally and enjoying the flamboyance of the arts world, she was actually quite a serious person at heart. Probably serious enough even to impress him. Far from being the tart that he obviously considered her, she had had only one love affair, and that had hurt her enough to steer her away from any other involvements. What was more, she would never in a million years have dreamt of marrying a naive boy like Tim just to get her hands on his money. It made her feel hot with rage all over again to realize that Matt thought her capable of such a thing. Well, I don't care what he thinks of me! she told herself, scowling defiantly. I just don't care!

'Everything all right?' Matt asked.

'Fine, thank you,' she said, forcing a smile.

Yet a faint sigh escaped her as the plane bumped along the runway, gathered speed and then suddenly lurched into flight. Everything wasn't all right, not by a long way. The man sitting next to her still seemed to radiate a dangerous magnetism that made her feel jumpy and uncomfortable. She wouldn't have worried so much about it if it hadn't been for his outrageous proposition the previous evening and the kiss that had followed. The knowledge that Matt wanted her just as badly as she wanted him made the whole situation perilously explosive. Lisa felt like a firewatcher, scanning a tinder-dry forest for the one spark that would set off a violent conflagration. Without Tim's presence to dampen down the tension between them, she felt an ominous certainty that they were headed for disaster. But what was she to do? She could see no obvious way out and she sat brooding silently over the problem until the plane levelled out and a smiling air hostess began to make her way down the aisle with a refreshment trolley.

'Smoked salmon sandwiches, madam?' she asked.

'Yes, please.'

'Don't eat too much,' warned Matt. 'I'm taking you to lunch at Eaglehawk Neck on the way to the farm.'

'Where is the farm?' asked Lisa curiously, suddenly realizing that she knew very little about this unfamiliar world she was about to enter.

'Didn't Tim tell you? It's on the Tasman Peninsula about one and a half hour's drive from the Hobart airport and about a million light-years away from Melbourne.'

He was right about that. As the glittering dark expanse of Bass Strait gave way to the rugged coastline of Tasmania and they flew over endless forests and mountains with scarcely a sign of human habitation, Lisa felt a strange thrill of expectancy. What was this place like that had produced two people as different as Matt Lansdon and his nephew Tim? Would it be like stepping into a time warp? Was it even possible that she might enjoy herself here? At last the roar of the engines changed and the plane began to tilt and plummet towards the earth. Pewter-grey seas and forest-clad hills tilted past the window at an alarming angle as the plane banked and turned for its approach to the runway. There was a screaming of engines, an uncomfortable pop in her ears, then a bump as the wheels touched ground and they taxied along the runway to land in front of the small terminal building. Here there were no space-age concertina tunnels, just a set of stairs and an exhilarating breeze, laden with the scent of sea air and eucalyptus, that sent Lisa's auburn hair flying around her shoulders. Within five minutes Matt had claimed their luggage and was glancing at his watch.

'Ready to go?' he asked.

'Aren't we going to wait for Tim?' she protested.

'There's no need for that. I'll leave a message at the Hertz desk to tell him to hire a car and drive home when he gets here.'

There was no reasonable objection that Lisa could make to this, but her uneasiness mounted as they went outside with their luggage on a trolley.

'How are we going to get to the farm?' she asked.

'I've left my car in the long-term car park. I generally do when I go over to Melbourne for a few days. It's the most convenient thing to do.'

He led the way to a glossy red Porsche and installed Lisa comfortably in the passenger seat before putting their bags in the boot and going to the office to pay for the parking ticket. As Lisa watched his powerful figure striding between the rows of parked cars, a faint smile strayed around the edges of her lips. Perhaps there was an advantage to old-fashioned men! Tim would probably have left it to her to handle both the bags and the payment. Not that he was at all mean, but he was incurably lazy, unlike his uncle. If Lisa had belonged to the world that Matt Lansdon inhabited, the world of old money and conservative values, would he have found her attractive? she wondered. Well, no, not just attractive. She knew already that he was attracted to her, but would he have liked her? Would he have taken her seriously? Would he have wanted her as his girlfriend without any insulting propositions about making her his mistress? She shook off these disturbing speculations as Matt came back, brandishing a parking ticket.

'Right, let's go.'

The airport was tiny and in less than a minute the car was turning down between an avenue of trees where rabbits frisked playfully on the grass and froze into attitudes of camouflage at the sound of each passing car.

As they turned on to the main road, the sun abruptly
broke from behind a cloud, illuminating the countryside.
The silver ribbons of water looped against the backdrop
of darker blue hills, shrouded in scarves of mist, suddenly gave way to a landscape that was almost tropical
in its brightness.

'Isn't the light amazing?' marvelled Lisa. 'And the
scenery is really dramatic, too. I'd love to do some
paintings here.'

'So you paint landscapes, do you?' asked Matt.

'Yes, it's the only thing I really have any talent for.
Of course, Tim's more interested in——' She broke off,
suddenly aware that she had said too much.

'Tim's more interested in?' prompted Matt.

'Oh, well. You know. Social life,' floundered Lisa.
'And accountancy. He's much more interested in
accountancy.'

'Is he, indeed? Well, that makes a change from his
past attitude to his studies. But never mind Tim. If you're
seriously interested in painting landscapes, we must stop
at the lookout at the entrance to the Tasman Peninsula.
I think you'll agree that the scenery there is nothing short
of spectacular.'

He was right, as Lisa soon discovered. When they
climbed out of the car in the deserted parking area and
strode to the lookout high over Pirates Bay, she gave a
low gasp of amazement. How could anyone ever capture
on canvas the immensity of that panorama? Craggy
headlands plummeted down into seething, dark blue seas,
while foaming breakers smashed against their bases.
There was a light scattering of holiday homes, but apart
from those, dense, jungly vegetation seemed to cover
every square inch of the land's surface, making the place
look mysterious, secret, primitive. Overhead seagulls

glided silently, their breast feathers flashing white against the dizzying blue enormity of the sky. The place looked untouched, unspoilt, almost as it must have looked to the first explorers who had faced the challenge of surviving and prospering in this beautiful terrifying environment with only their own hard work and resourcefulness to support them.

For the first time she felt a flash of insight into the character of Matt Lansdon. Yes, she could see him as one of those pioneers. Arrogant and conservative perhaps, but also strong and determined, the kind of man a woman could depend on. An odd little shiver travelled up Lisa's spine. Depend on? Why was she turning so mushy? In the past she had always had to depend on herself. Matt's words suddenly broke into her thoughts.

'If you want to see some more of the countryside, I could take you on a tour around the whole peninsula tomorrow.'

'Thank you,' said Lisa, stepping back a pace. 'But I'm sure Tim will do that.'

'Oh, Tim,' he murmured, swallowing a smile. 'Tim. Yes, I suppose he might.'

Lisa's suspicions came clamouring back as he escorted her to the car. Matt didn't sound as if he expected to see Tim for a very long time. What was he up to? Could she trust him?

The hotel was set high on a bank overlooking the sea. A smiling young man showed them to a table with a panoramic view of the tossing waves whose colours seemed to change moment by moment with the shifting light from emerald to sapphire to a pale, lavender grey.

'Can I get you some drinks, sir?' he asked.

'Lisa? Something to drink?'

'A sweet vermouth with ginger ale, please.'

'And I'll have a gin and tonic.'

'Certainly. I'll bring you those in a moment. And our food menu is on a blackboard in the bar.'

A dangerous sense of well-being and relaxation began to spread through Lisa's veins as she sipped the sweet, tingling drink.

'Tell me, what kind of food do you like?' asked Matt lazily.

Lisa took a deep breath, as if she was inhaling all the aromas of a master chef's kitchen.

'Every kind,' she said. 'The more exotic, the better. Things like octopus and goat's cheese. Vegetarian food, for preference.'

'That makes sense,' said Matt, nodding his head sagely.

'Why?' challenged Lisa.

'Well, you can tell a lot about people from what they eat. Yes, I would have picked you as an octopus person. Adventurous, sensation-seeking, unconventional.'

Lisa gazed back at him stormily. Somehow he made those qualities sound vaguely indecent.

'What do you like to eat?' she countered. 'Roast lamb, steak and kidney pudding?'

'No, those are too hard on my teeth,' replied Matt in a deadpan voice. 'I prefer a nice bowl of porridge and a cup of Horlicks.'

Lisa gave a sudden startled gasp of laughter. She hadn't thought Matt Lansdon was capable of irony.

'I'm sorry,' she said penitently. 'You seem so stern and conservative, it's hard to believe you could ever joke about anything. Anyway, I'm sure the roast lamb or whatever they serve will be very nice.'

'You underestimate us,' said Matt. 'You may be surprised when you find out what sophistication lurks beneath our conservative exterior around these parts. Come over and see what's available.'

He steered her into the bar and watched with an ironic smile as she read the choices aloud from the blackboard.

'Anchovies with sun-dried tomato mayonnaise, grilled emu, guinea fowl marinated in lemon and garlic, brown mushroom ragout, polenta with capsicum, octopus and goat's milk cheese...oops, I take it all back. I did underestimate you. But there's no need to smirk at me in that obnoxious way. What are you going to have?'

'Grilled emu,' replied Matt.

Fifteen minutes later Lisa sat quietly studying her companion as he began eating his unusual meal. She was beginning to suspect that Tim had seriously misrepresented his uncle. From her flatmate's descriptions, she had pictured Matt Lansdon as a ferocious, pigheaded old grouch with the narrow outlook of a nineteenth-century pioneer. Instead he had proved to be relatively young and disturbingly sensual and was now revealing unexpected depths of sophistication. Of course, she would never in a million years have expected to have lunch with a man like this, but she could not deny that she found him intriguing. As she savoured the diverse textures and subtle flavours of the chewy octopus and creamy goat's cheese, Lisa forgot that she was suffering a nerve-racking ordeal at the hands of a merciless tormentor and began to enjoy herself.

'So where did you acquire your taste for octopus?' asked Matt. 'In Melbourne, or somewhere more exotic?'

'The Greek islands,' replied Lisa with her mouth full. 'My mother was renting a villa in the Dodecanese about four years ago and I stayed with her for a while. I'll never forget those wonderful moonlit nights on the vine-covered terrace, with bouzouki music playing in the background and people strolling around in the streets of the village down below. And, of course, the food. Kebabs, grilled cheese, octopus. I loved it.'

'What was your mother doing there?' asked Matt with interest.

'She's a university lecturer. She was away on sabbatical leave,' replied Lisa.

'So you come from an academic background? That surprises me. And how does your mother view your present way of life?'

'Oh, she disapproves of me!' said Lisa cheerfully.

Matt's eyebrows peaked. 'I can see her point.'

'Can you? I doubt it. The reason she disapproves of me is that she thinks I'm too conservative.'

'Too conservative?' echoed Matt, aghast.

Lisa grinned wickedly at his discomfiture.

'Yes. She's a lecturer in women's studies. She used to be a hippy back in the seventies and she's always telling me that I should get in touch with my natural impulses.'

'Has Tim met your parents?' he growled.

'Why should Tim——' began Lisa. 'Oh, no, not really. Well, I haven't met my father all that often myself, and my mother lives in Sydney, you see. But she's fairly un-maternal. We're more like friends really, rather than mother and daughter. I've always called her by her first name—Suzanne—and she'd have the cold horrors at the thought of inspecting any of my boyfriends to see if they were suitable for marrying. She just takes it for granted that I'll do whatever I choose and tell her about it afterwards.'

Disapproval showed in every line of Matt's face.

'What about your father?' he demanded abruptly. 'Why haven't you met him very often?'

'Oh, he's American and he's always lived in the United States. My mother met him when she went there to do her Masters degree in history about thirty years ago. They dropped out for a while and joined a commune and they were into Haight-Ashbury and Woodstock, all that sort of thing. Suzanne became pregnant and Ralph, that's my father, turned really conservative. He went back to join his father's law firm and he talked her into marrying him, but it made her feel trapped. The marriage only lasted three years, then they split up. Suzanne came back to Australia with my brother Brian and me, and Ralph's still in the United States. I didn't really meet him properly until I was twenty-one and I've only seen him a couple of times since.'

'Brian and Lisa?' mused Matt. 'Those are surprisingly conservative names for a hippy mother, aren't they?'

A dimple showed in Lisa's cheek.

'Well, she wanted to call us Alpha and Night Star, but my father wouldn't let her.'

'Your father sounds like a man after my own heart,' muttered Matt. 'Quite frankly, I can't imagine why women like that bother to have children.'

'Don't criticize her!' flared Lisa. 'At least she loved us, which is more than my father did, or he would have tried to contact us all those years that we were living out here. And Suzanne always kept us with her, no matter how much she moved around or who she lived with. She didn't shove us off to boarding school the way Sonia did with poor old Tim.'

Matt's eyes narrowed at the mention of his nephew's name.

'You think it was wrong to send Tim to boarding school, do you?'

'Yes. He hated the place and I think you're just as bad as Sonia for letting it happen. Both of you just want him to act out the script that you've written for him and you won't let him be an individual. I think it's wrong for families to imprint their requirements on kids. They should let them discover themselves.'

'Did you discover yourself while you were traipsing around after your mother?' asked Matt sceptically.

Lisa was silent for a moment, staring abstractedly out the window as if she were watching some procession from the past.

'Yes, I did,' she said at last.

'And what exactly did you discover?'

'What's the use of telling you? You'll only sneer at me, whatever I say.'

His eyes met hers with that disconcerting blue gaze.

'Tell me,' he urged.

'I found out that I liked the warmth and spontaneity of my mother's way of life,' said Lisa, tossing her head. 'Even though I didn't like the drifting or the lack of continuity, I found out that I do accept some of her values. But the really important thing that I found out was that I love her and won't sit here and listen to you condemn her when you know nothing about her.'

Matt suddenly dropped his eyes and his mouth tightened. Then he looked up at her with a grudging nod of approval.

'You're quite right,' he said unexpectedly. 'And I admire you for it. Family loyalty is very important to me, too. Will you accept my apology for criticizing your mother?'

Lisa was taken aback by this unexpected tact and sincerity. For a moment she felt a rush of goodwill towards Matt, a dangerous feeling that she could lay everything before him and he would understand. Not just the childish deception that she had concocted with Tim, but all her past hopes and disappointments and insecurities, all the dreams she cherished for the rest of her life. In spite of his stern exterior, she felt he would really listen to her. She opened her mouth as if to speak and then paused. Was she out of her mind? How could she possibly trust him?

'Yes, I accept your apology,' she muttered.

Later, as they were lingering over a delicious tangerine meringue and hot, fragrant black coffee, Matt turned the conversation back to her family.

'You said you had a brother,' he reminded her. 'What does he do?'

'He's an actor,' said Lisa with a touch of defiance. 'You've probably seen him on TV. Brian Hayward. He played a cocaine addict in one of those medical series last year on the ABC.'

To her surprise Matt did not utter any scathing comment, but merely nodded.

'Yes, I did see him. He was very talented. I think I also saw him in a production of *The Revenger's Tragedy* in Sydney two or three years ago.'

Lisa's eyes widened in surprise. 'Are you interested in the theatre?' she asked.

'Is there any reason I shouldn't be?'

'No. I suppose not. It's just that Tim gave me the impression that you were only interested in the farm and making money.'

'The farm was going through a very difficult stage when my brother died,' growled Matt. 'I had to be interested in both of those things if the entire family was not to go broke and after a few years the hard work and the preoccupation became a habit. But that doesn't make me a complete boor! Still, you're probably right to criticize me for not taking more interest in Tim's education. I should have spent more time with the boy when he was in high school. As it is, I hardly know anything about him.'

Lisa was touched by this admission of his own failings.

'Well, I think you ought to know that he doesn't want to be a farmer and that he's not interested in finance,' she said softly.

'Maybe not,' replied Matt with a flash of the old arrogance that antagonized her. 'But he's going to inherit a lot of money and land in a few years' time and he needs to know how to deal with it so nobody can fleece him. If he had shown any signs of being seriously attracted to another profession, I might have considered allowing him to train for it. As it is, I believe I'm doing the best I can for him.'

'What about you? Did you always want to be a farmer?' asked Lisa.

'No, but that's the way it turned out and I'm not complaining. Now, should we go for a walk along the beach to settle our lunch?'

They were just leaving the hotel when they caught sight of a woman of about Matt's age coming towards them. She was small and slightly built with feathery blonde curls, green eyes and a rather strained expression on her face. She wore a stylish, pale green linen dress and carried a cane shopping basket over one arm. With her other hand she was tugging a small boy of about four who kept trying to break away from her and run back towards the path that led to the shore. The woman's face lit up

at the sight of Matt and she immediately hurried forward
and kissed him. Lisa saw a strange expression flit across
his face, a mixture of pity, affection and exasperation,
which was gone in an instant. He turned to Lisa and
made the necessary introductions.

'Andrea, I'd like you to meet Lisa Hayward, who has
come over from Melbourne as my guest. Lisa, this is my
old friend Andrea Spencer and her son, Justin.'

Lisa suffered a double shock. First there was the brief
but unmistakable flare of dismay in Andrea's eyes, which
was swiftly hidden. Yet worse than that was the jolt that
went through Lisa herself as she looked down at the small
boy who was now clutching at Matt's leg and gazing
adoringly up at him. The child was the image of Matt,
right down to the cleft in his chin. With his dark hair,
light blue eyes and imperious mouth, he was like a
miniature version of the man to whom he clung. In any
other circumstances Lisa would have identified him un-
hesitatingly as Matt's son. But Matt was un-
married... of course, that didn't necessarily mean that
the child wasn't his. Suddenly Lisa felt as if someone
had punched her in the stomach. A sickening sensation
of betrayal and jealousy left her unable to speak for a
moment. Then, glancing from the child to Andrea, she
found her own emotions mirrored on the other woman's
face. Anger, distress, apprehension. Lisa almost reeled
at the intensity of her feelings, but immediately struggled
to regain her poise. If what she suspected was true,
Andrea had far better reason than she did for such a
reaction. After all, Lisa had no claim on Matt. So why
should she feel so horrified at the thought that he might
have fathered another woman's child?

'Hello, Andrea,' she said, trying to infuse some
warmth into the greeting. 'Hello, Justin.'

Andrea's recovery was quick, Lisa had to give her that. She smiled politely and held out her hand.

'Hello, Lisa,' she murmured. 'Are you staying here long?'

Before Lisa could reply Matt intervened.

'She's staying indefinitely,' he said.

The stricken look returned to Andrea's face, but her courtesy didn't waver.

'Well, Justin and I had better get moving,' she continued in a high, rapid voice, blinking twice. 'We only came to buy some soft drinks for his party on Saturday. He's turning four, you remember. You will call in if you can make it, won't you, Matt?'

Matt gave her a wry smile that seemed indescribably cruel to Lisa.

'Of course, Andrea. If I can make it,' he agreed in a voice that suggested he had no intention of doing so. 'It was nice seeing you both. Goodbye, Justin. Buy some chips, if Mum will let you.'

Matt fished in his pocket and pressed a coin into the child's hand. Justin grinned up at him, his smile so like Matt's that Lisa could hardly bear to look.

'Goodbye, Matt.' Andrea's voice came out as little more than a husky whisper. 'Goodbye, Lisa. I hope you enjoy your stay.'

As they walked to the Porsche, Lisa was attacked by two conflicting impulses, both equally powerful. To burst into tears or to punch Matt Lansdon in the nose, good and hard. A great wave of irrational guilt and pity broke over her as she glanced over her shoulder at Andrea. But why should she feel guilty? Even if her suspicions were true, she wasn't attempting to steal Matt from Andrea. She hadn't done anything. Then the memory of that kiss in the elevator of the State Theatre came surging back.

To her shame she felt anew the tingling flame of excitement that had filled her then. Well, I didn't know he was involved with someone else, she told herself defensively. Besides, it doesn't look as though he is involved any more. But that bleak thought didn't bring her any comfort. She certainly had no intention of falling in love with a man who would callously desert the mother of his own child. Wait a minute, Lisa! she almost shouted at herself. Who said anything about falling in love with Matt Lansdon? You'd better watch your step, girl.

It only made her hate Matt more than ever to realize that he seemed quite impervious to either her troubled silence or Andrea's barely concealed distress. He held the car door open for Lisa with the faint, mocking smile that infuriated her.

'We'll just drive down a little farther so we can get access to the beach,' he said.

He parked the car in a spot behind the sand dunes and they picked their way down a set of silvery wooden steps between the high banks of marram grass. The beach was deserted, its fine, powdery white sand marked only by the ripples of wind and waves and the delicate footprints of sea birds. But Lisa took little pleasure in the vast expanse of aquamarine water, the crashing surf, the wracks of leathery brown kelp or the tangy salt air. Her mind was preoccupied with other things.

'Have you known Andrea long?'

'All my life.'

'Does she work on the Tasman Peninsula?'

'She used to. She was a schoolteacher. But she stopped when Justin was born and she hasn't been able to get another job.'

'What does her husband do?' asked Lisa in a carefully casual voice.

'She hasn't got a husband. She's a single mother,' replied Matt curtly.

Lisa felt a sickening lurch as if she had just looked over the edge of a cliff.

'That must be hard for her,' she said accusingly.

Matt shrugged.

'I imagine it is,' he retorted. 'But she went into the situation with her eyes open, so she can hardly complain.'

You swine, thought Lisa. She was far too angry now to have any scruples about being nosy.

'What about the child's father?' she asked.

'What about him? Is it really any of your business?'

Lisa seethed quietly at the rudeness of this reply and the callous insensitivity that seemed to lie behind it.

'No, I suppose not,' she admitted grudgingly.

'Good. Then can we stop talking about Andrea? Look, have you ever seen those pied oystercatchers before? Colourful little creatures, aren't they?'

Lisa tried to pretend an interest in the black and white birds with their vivid red legs and beaks that were hunting for food in the shallows, but her thoughts were elsewhere. She barely looked at the jellyfish or the shells or the huge boulders of porous rock that littered the beach. Her mind was racing with indignation as she tramped along beside Matt on the firm sand near the water's edge. Tim was right, she thought, darting a glance at the powerful, ruthless male striding along beside her, his dark hair blowing wildly in the sea breeze. He's nothing but a domineering, insensitive brute. The sooner I leave this place, the better!

'You do think Tim will arrive this afternoon, don't you?' she asked anxiously.

'Yes, of course,' said Matt in a bland voice that somehow made her feel more uneasy than ever. 'Why shouldn't he?'

'Then can we go to the farm now? I want to make sure I'm there when he comes.'

'Dear me, how impatient you young lovers are,' drawled Matt. 'It's only a few hours since you left him. Why are you so eager to see him again?'

So I can persuade him to take me back to the airport, thought Lisa grimly. Or so I can hijack his rental car and drive myself there if necessary. But she didn't say this. She simply gave Matt a wide-eyed, dreamy smile.

'Because we've never been parted before, and I already miss him such a lot,' she said in a syrupy voice.

'I think I'm going to be sick,' growled Matt.

The farm was situated a few miles from the old convict ruins at Saltwater River. It was set high on a grassy hillside with panoramic views over a sapphire blue bay and vast white tidal flats. As they turned up the dirt road Lisa saw red and white Hereford cattle grazing knee-deep in the lush grass while in other paddocks half-grown lambs frisked in the shelter of hawthorn hedges. Three or four horses raised their heads to watch the passage of the car, and when they came up the last curve of fawn, dusty road, a chorus of barking rose from the dog kennels beside the stables. Matt drew the car to a halt and helped Lisa out.

'Well, here you are,' he said with a touch of irony. 'Your first glimpse of your new home.'

Lisa felt a pang of excitement as she looked around her. I wish it were! she thought breathlessly. It's such a beautiful old place. The house looked exactly like a doll's house that Lisa had once yearned for as a child. It was built in the Victorian Gothic style with steeply pitched gables, dormer windows and decoratively carved barge-boards. A veranda trimmed with white iron lace extended along two sides of the building, and it stood right in the middle of a lush, green garden. A massive, clipped box hedge ran around the perimeter and within its shelter grew masses of brightly coloured flowers. Orange calendulas, tall, pink, nodding foxgloves, tangled yellow roses, vivid blue lobelias and red geraniums. But Matt gave her little time to sniff the warm, sweet, flowery scents or to explore the nooks and crannies of the garden. Lifting his expensive pigskin suitcase and Lisa's battered backpack out of the boot, he strode briskly across to a side door.

'Come in and get settled,' he ordered. 'My housekeeper usually leaves by three o'clock, but I can phone her at her cottage if there's anything you need.'

Gazing around with barely concealed curiosity, Lisa followed him through the French doors into a large room furnished with deep leather couches and imposing mahogany bookcases crammed with books. Her reflection glanced at her easily from the huge, gilt mirror above the carved mantelpiece. She felt like an impostor, a confidence trickster, someone who had lied her way into this place and was now at a loss to know what to do. Matt's reflection suddenly joined her in the mirror, but he looked completely self-assured. Mocking, arrogant, totally in control of the situation.

'I suppose you'd like me to show you over the house,' he suggested. 'After all, it will be your home if you marry Tim.'

A creepy feeling of unreality made Lisa's skin rise in goose bumps. This whole ridiculous game was becoming far too much for her to handle. Illusion and reality blurred for an instant as she stared at the silvery glass. For one wild moment she did picture herself living here, not with Tim, but with Matt....

'No!' she exclaimed in an unnaturally loud voice, turning away from the mirror and breaking the spell. 'No...thank you. That won't be necessary. Anyway...I suppose Tim will want to do it when he comes.'

Matt shrugged. 'Just as you like. I'll show you to your room at any rate.'

Matt had just ushered her into a beautifully decorated bedroom with a half tester bed and flower-sprigged green and white wallpaper when the telephone rang. Suppressing an urge to snatch at it, Lisa stood watching hopefully as Matt picked up the receiver.

'Hello? Yes, sure. About an hour?'

'Is it Tim?' she whispered.

He shook his head, spoke a few more cryptic sentences and replaced the receiver.

'No. It's my farm manager, Ron Barwick. I hope you'll excuse me for an hour or so. There's some urgent business I must deal with. Just make yourself at home until I come back.'

Left alone, Lisa sat down on the bed and groaned. This is worse than final exams, she thought. I can't stand too much more of it. When is Tim going to arrive? A sudden inspiration struck her and she reached for the telephone. If she knew the flight arrival times, at least she could calculate when he should reach the farm. With shaking fingers, she dialled.

'Arriving four-twenty, six-twenty and ten o'clock? Thank you.' She put down the receiver and frowned thoughtfully as she looked at her watch. Almost four-thirty, but the drive from the airport took an hour and a half. With luck Tim should be here by six o'clock and she could find some way to leave!

Six o'clock came and went. She and Matt were drinking sherry at the time and he seemed quite unconscious of the way her gaze kept straying to her watch. Or of the eagerness with which she jumped to her feet when the sound of a car engine came up the dirt road... and continued straight past the entrance to the homestead. At eight o'clock, when she began to tense in readiness for the next likely arrival, he was equally calm, offering her a second helping of beef stew or some apple pie with cream. Only at nearly midnight, when they were sitting in the living room gazing into the glowing orange flames at the heart of the fire, did he turn to her with a pitying smile.

'I know this must be a terrible blow to you, Lisa,' he murmured. 'But isn't it time to admit that your fiancé is not coming?'

CHAPTER FOUR

'I'D LIKE to hit you,' snapped Lisa, annoyed by his gloating tone.

'Why?' he asked mildly. 'For stating the truth? It seems pretty obvious now that Tim wasn't nearly so deeply entangled as you hoped if he's prepared to run off and leave you. So why don't you just call it quits and break the engagement?'

Lisa's eyes flashed. Even though the engagement had never existed, except as a fantasy, she couldn't bear to let Matt have the satisfaction of feeling he had won. Instead she hit back.

'No,' she flared. 'If anybody's going to persuade me to do that, it will be Tim, not you. Still, if my presence is embarrassing to you, I'll be happy to leave on the first flight tomorrow.'

Matt seemed to undergo a disconcertingly swift change of mood. His dark eyebrows drew together in a thoughtful frown and he suddenly shook his head.

'Look,' he said with a rueful smile. 'Perhaps I've misjudged you, Lisa. It's entirely possible that you and I got off on the wrong foot and, if so, it could be my fault. But I don't want you to leave because of it.' He sighed and looked down at his fingernails. 'You've been accusing me of not taking enough interest in Tim, and perhaps you're right. It could be that this marriage with you will be exactly what he needs. I know you don't love him, but love isn't the only basis for a good marriage. Affection can be important, too, and you did say you were fond of him. Well, if you do decide to go ahead with it, I suppose I'll just have to wish you all the luck in the world.'

Lisa was taken aback by Matt's sudden change of attitude. Suddenly he sounded so nice, so decent, so caring that a lump rose in her throat and she surreptitiously reached for her handkerchief and blew her nose. It made her feel so guilty to hear him talk like this that she hovered on the verge of confessing everything. Then Matt continued.

'I think you should stay on here. After all, if you and I are going to be related, we should get to know each other. It's really our duty to try to be friends.'

'Friends?' demanded Lisa suspiciously. Suddenly warning bells seemed to be clamouring in her head. Bells that shrieked alarm, danger, red alert. 'I hope this doesn't mean that you're going to...going to——'

'Proposition you again?' asked Matt in a shocked voice. 'Lisa, you're being too hard on me. Besides, if I did a thing like that, you'd know what to say to me, wouldn't you?'

He took a few lazy, catlike paces across the floor and stood gazing down at her with an unfathomable expression. Her heart began to race and she felt breathless, on the point of suffocating. His nearness, the spicy, masculine smell of him were making her head swim. For one crazy moment she wanted to fling herself into his arms and feel that powerful, masculine grip tighten around her and let him kiss her, savagely, thrillingly, as he had kissed her at the State Theatre. Nervously she stepped back a pace and then her head jerked up and her eyes flashed fire.

'You can bet your life I'd know what to tell you,' she hissed.

'Good. Then you're in no danger,' he murmured. 'You can just stay here and enjoy painting the scenery and planning out your married life. Or don't you have the guts to stay?'

Earlier in the evening, Lisa had been sure of only one thing. That she wanted to get away from this place and this man at any cost. But now she found the old childhood taunt was as inflammatory as ever. *Go on, I dare you!* A hot flame of rage surged through her and made her eyes sparkle angrily as she looked at Matt.

'Yes, I have got the guts to do it!' she retorted. 'Provided you've got the decency not to take advantage of me while I'm under your roof.'

'Take advantage of you? Now there's an antiquated phrase. But don't worry, sweetheart. There's no question of my taking advantage of you. Anything that happens between us will happen with your full consent.'

Lisa awoke the next morning feeling much as she had felt before her first overseas trip when she was twenty years old. That same simmering mixture of excitement and apprehension was churning her stomach. But why? She wasn't about to launch herself into the unknown right now. Or was she? All the turbulent emotions of the previous evening came flooding back to her and she caught her breath. Was she crazy to have accepted Matt's challenge to stay here on the farm? And why had she accepted? Perhaps because she was naturally rash and impulsive? Or perhaps because the landscapes on this peninsula really did cry out to be painted. Or perhaps because Matt Lansdon intrigued her so much that she couldn't bear to walk out of his life without getting to know just a little more about him....

You're playing with fire, Lisa! she warned herself, as she flung back the patchwork quilt and climbed out of bed. He's not the kind of man you can play games with— you'll wind up getting hurt. Look at what happened with Saul Oakley. Her thoughts went to the producer at the small, experimental theatre in upstate New York where she had spent an unforgettable summer four years ago. The image of Saul's lean, saturnine face with the long creases in the cheeks and the slow, devastating smile flashed before her. She waited for the stab of pain that always accompanied the memory in the past, but for some reason it didn't come. Instead she felt a flare of exasperation. Saul really was a manipulative brute, she thought irritably. The way he used to tell me that I was a really special person and that my performances on stage were so amazingly fresh and moving! I can't believe that I swallowed all his flattery and went to bed with him! How could I have been such a fool? But I really thought he loved me. And all the time he had a wife and two children back in Boston. Well, I'm not a gullible twenty-one-year-old any more, so Matt Lansdon had better not try any of those smooth-talking tricks on me!

Yet when she came down to breakfast, Matt showed no sign of even looking at her, much less playing tricks on her. He was sitting at the head of the vast mahogany table in the dining room, frowning thoughtfully at the financial pages of a newspaper. His only acknowledgment of her presence was a curt grunt and a vague wave of the hand at the sideboard where several silver chafing dishes stood over blue-flamed spirit lamps.

'Help yourself to some breakfast,' he ordered. 'I have to make a phone call.'

Lisa felt rather piqued as she lifted the covers from the dishes, revealing an array of sausages, bacon, grilled

tomatoes, fried bread and scrambled eggs. It wasn't that
she wanted him to notice her new jade green slacks and
blouse, she told herself hastily, just that she thought he
was very rude to grunt at people. As she took her place
at the side of the table, she stole a glance at Matt. He
was wearing an open-necked blue checked shirt, rolled
up to the elbows, and fawn moleskin trousers. With his
stern jaw, narrowed eyes and tanned, muscular body he
looked as if he had just come inside after riding hundreds
of miles on the range. But his conversation was not about
cattle, it was about finance. He scowled at the phone in
his left hand and rapped out a set of incomprehensible
figures. At last with an approving nod, he set down the
receiver and put the phone back on the sideboard.

'Sorry about that,' he said, looking at Lisa for the
first time. 'I had to catch my money market dealer.
Eleven o'clock money, you know.'

Lisa blinked. 'Oh,' she said in a baffled voice.

Matt grinned suddenly.

'I'll explain it to you one of these days,' he promised.
'In the meantime, take it from me that you can make a
lot of money by making the right phone calls before
eleven. Now why don't you eat your breakfast and then
we'll do our little tour of the peninsula.'

It was a fine day outside, but Lisa was too absorbed
in her turbulent responses to take much notice of the
new experiences that were assailing her. She was only
dimly aware of her surroundings. The clean, aromatic
scent of the air as they emerged from the house, the
sound of magpies warbling in the trees, the jade green
seas crashing on the beaches, the glossy stands of eucalyptus trees with their red-tipped new growth barely pen-
etrated her consciousness. All her senses were focused
far too acutely on the powerful stranger who sat beside

her, guiding the car over the rough roads with deceptive ease and occasionally casting her sly, sideways glances. What was he thinking? Why was he looking at her with that amused, penetrating scrutiny? As they drove through the tiny village of Nubeena, Lisa was suddenly startled out of her speculation by the sight of a large mailbox near the roadside with the name Spencer written on it in capital letters.

'Is that Andrea's house?' she blurted out before she could stop herself.

'Yes.'

Matt's face took on a shut, secretive expression, and his clipped tone did not invite any further questions.

'I thought we'd go to Remarkable Cave first,' he said after a long pause. 'And after that we can visit the convict ruins at Port Arthur.'

Lisa's feelings were in turmoil as she climbed out of the car at the cliff top overlooking Remarkable Cave. Whatever was going on between Matt and Andrea, it was none of her business. So why should it upset her so much? Why did she feel this bewildering surge of resentment, jealousy and compassion? Why did she feel so sorry for Andrea and Justin and at the same time wish that they had never existed? She scowled at Matt as he came around the front of the car to join her.

'Are you wearing flat heels?' he asked. 'Good. You don't suffer from vertigo, do you?'

'No.'

'Well, I'll go ahead of you down the stairs just in case. It's a long fall to the foot of the cliff.'

Lisa saw what he meant when she followed him across the road to the start of the track. Dense flowering bushes hung over the path and it gave her an eerie feeling of solitude to realize that there were no other human beings in sight. With one of the abrupt changes of weather that seemed so characteristic of this island, the earlier sunshine had given way to scudding, charcoal grey clouds. The hills looked bleak and lonely, and far below the hidden sea moaned and thundered on the rocks. Lizards scuttled beneath their feet as they picked their way down the weathered wooden stairs, twisting and turning in a series of landings. Suddenly the cove came into view beneath them and Lisa saw that there was a small, rock-strewn beach reached by a sea cave through which the water came surging down a long, dark tunnel. Cautiously she followed Matt down the last flight of stairs onto the rocky beach and looked around her. Here the hiss and suck of the waves was almost deafening with the noise echoing back along the tunnel that led to the open sea. As a painter, she was intrigued by the atmosphere of the place. There was something eerie, almost ominous about it, with the low grinding noise of the rocks being rolled back by the pounding waves, the grey fleeting clouds overhead and the lonely cry of a sea bird wheeling above the sheer cliffs. Yet somehow Matt's presence reassured her. If anything went wrong, she thought, he would take care of me. He'd even carry me up that steep staircase if I was hurt. She gazed at his muscular physique, his narrowed blue eyes and the stern set of his jaw and felt an odd, pleasurable flutter deep inside her. Yes, Matt Lansdon was the kind of man you could rely on. Then the fluttering sensation was followed by a deep ache, as if a cold hand had clutched her heart. Andrea Spencer hadn't been able to rely on him, had she?

'Seen enough?' asked Matt.

She nodded silently and made her way across the smooth silver stones that littered the beach. As she climbed up the endless staircase towards the road, she was very careful not to slip or stumble. She didn't want to give Matt Lansdon any excuse for carrying her! Her breath was coming in deep burning gulps and her legs were aching when at last they came out on to the cliff top. Lisa paused for a moment, inhaling the mingled scents of aromatic leaves and cool, salt air.

'Whew!' she gasped. 'I'd love a cup of tea.'

'I thought you might say that,' said Matt in amusement. 'I'll get you one.'

He went to the car and returned with a silver Thermos flask and two china mugs.

'Hold these,' he ordered as he unscrewed the flask.

Lisa gave an involuntary exclamation of delight as she sipped the sweet, fragrant lemon-scented tea.

'Oh, just the way I like it. How did you know?'

'It wasn't difficult. I noticed what you ordered on the plane.'

'That was thoughtful of you.'

She flashed him a troubled look as she took another sip of the hot, sweet tea. Yes, it had been thoughtful of him, but perversely she wished he hadn't bothered. His attentiveness to her comfort disturbed her. She knew perfectly well that he was hard and tough and ruthless and it only confused her to find that he was considerate, as well. A renewed sense of misgiving overtook her. Why had Matt asked her to stay on here? She couldn't believe his glib explanation that they ought to get to know each other because they were soon going to be relatives! Wasn't it far more likely that he simply intended to try to seduce her? Hastily she gulped down the last of the tea and handed back the empty cup with a despairing expression as if she had just drained a poison chalice. Matt's eyes met hers and something sparked between them, something that made her shiver. For a moment she thought he was going to reach out and take her in his arms and she almost wished that he would try to kiss her, so that she could have the satisfaction of hating him, of knowing what he was after. But he didn't. He simply took the cup from her fingers and gave her an odd, twisted smile.

'I like that green outfit,' he said in an offhand tone. 'The colour suits you.'

Then he turned back to the car. Lisa's senses were clamouring as they drove towards Port Arthur. If Matt had touched her, what would she have done? Would she have made some sarcastic remark about Andrea? Or would she have let him go ahead and kiss her, despising him as he did so and despising herself for allowing it? Or would she have flung caution to the winds and responded passionately, just as she had done in the lift the night before last? Not caring whether he was reliable or sincere but caring only that he made her burn with desire in a way that she had never experienced before? She glanced across at him and shuddered. I must have been mad to stay on there, she thought despairingly. I've never felt like this about a man before. Never. Never! But I don't trust Matt Lansdon as far as I can throw him. I must get away from him.

'Do you think Tim will arrive today?' she asked in a high, nervous voice.

Matt shrugged indifferently.

'Perhaps. We can go home and check once you've seen Port Arthur.'

The sun had come out again by the time they drove down the winding road between the old sandstone ruins, but Lisa found it hard to keep her mind on the vista of blue sea, green rolling lawns and abandoned buildings.

And, in spite of her claim that she wanted to draw landscapes, the only sketch she did was not of a landscape at all. When Matt produced a hamper and began unpacking the excellent picnic provided by his housekeeper, Lisa reached into her bag for her sketchpad, and her pencil flew across the paper. Yes, there he was, captured to the life—the tense, thoughtful stance, the brooding eyebrows, the hint of danger in the narrowed eyes, the tough, ironic mouth. Suddenly Matt's lean, brown fingers plucked the pad out of her hand.

'What have we here?' he asked mildly.

Lisa held her breath as he scrutinized the portrait. Only now did she see its resemblance to some bird of prey—a hovering raptor awaiting its chance to swoop on a victim and destroy it.

Matt let out a harsh growl of laughter.

'You've made me look like a hawk,' he complained. 'Still, you certainly have talent. I recognize myself in this. May I keep it?'

'Y-yes, of course,' stammered Lisa. 'But I didn't mean to be insulting.'

His eyes met hers, blue, pitiless, challenging.

'Never apologize for telling the truth. You've captured me exactly as I am. A predator that swoops down on fluffy little bunnies. You'd be wise to remember it. Now let's have something to eat.'

His warning still rang in her ears as she ate lobster salad with brown bread and a glass of Tasmanian Riesling, followed by strawberries and cream and heavenly chocolate truffles. The whole situation made her feel fluttery and unsettled. Matt Lansdon didn't even attempt to conceal his own vices, and she had no doubt that plenty of other women had found themselves in his clutches like fluffy little bunnies. If she had any sense, she would run for her life instead of feeling this dangerous thrill of excitement in his company. She must escape before something disastrous happened.

'Do you think Tim would be back yet?' she bleated, as if she was holding up a talisman to ward off a vampire.

Matt's black eyebrows peaked and he gazed at her lazily from under half-closed eyelids.

'It's interesting how you seem to see Tim as some kind of protector,' he remarked. 'Someone who will save you from the dangers of my company. Am I really so fearsome? Or is it just that you're more in love with Tim than you've admitted to me so far?'

Lisa gazed at him in alarm. His questions were far too probing and she felt as if she was skating on very thin ice.

'Can't we go back?' she begged. 'Can't we see if he's home yet?'

But when they arrived at the farm, Tim wasn't home. Matt surveyed the empty turning circle next to the garage with unconcealed amusement.

'Dear me,' he drawled. 'There doesn't seem to be any sign of my dauntless nephew or his rental car, does there? But perhaps Judy Barwick has seen him.'

He led Lisa into the house where a grey-haired woman in a flowered overall stopped vigorously polishing the hall stand in order to greet them. Matt smiled at her.

'Lisa, this is my housekeeper, Judy Barwick. Lisa's staying on as my guest for a while, Judy. Tell me, has there been any news of my nephew Tim? He didn't arrive on the lunchtime plane by any chance, did he?'

Judy shook her head. 'No, Matt, he didn't.'

Lisa felt an odd mixture of relief and disappointment at this announcement.

'Well, did he telephone and explain what's delaying him?' she burst out.

The housekeeper shook her head again. 'No,' she said with a puzzled frown. 'But there was a letter from him in the mail addressed to you, Matt. It was in one of those express delivery envelopes. I put it on your desk in the study.'

Lisa followed Matt into the study and watched anxiously as he opened the envelope. He took out a thick wad of typed documents and a single scrawled sheet of paper and scanned them with an indifferent expression.

'What does it say?' asked Lisa impatiently.

'See for yourself.'

He handed her the note. With a feeling of growing apprehension, Lisa began to read aloud.

'Dear Uncle Matt. Sorry—missed the plane. Thought the lease agreement might be urgent, so I'm posting it to you. Can't make it to Tasmania right now, but will come as soon as I can—by Christmas at the latest. Give my love to Lisa.'

Lisa was so furious that for a moment she could only gargle helplessly as if she had choked on a large mouthful of seawater. Damn Tim! Damn him! Did he always have to run out on difficult situations?

'Are you all right?' asked Matt solicitously.

'No,' she shouted at last. 'What on earth is Tim playing at? Christmas! That's five weeks away. I can't stay here alone with you for five weeks!'

A glint of amusement flashed in Matt's eyes.

'I've no objections,' he said suavely.

'Well, I have!' snapped Lisa. Belatedly she remembered her manners. 'I'm sorry, that sounded rude. I appreciate your invitation, but you must see that it makes no sense at all for me to be here without Tim.'

'Why not?' asked Matt. 'If you're going to marry Tim, there are times when you'll be here on the farm without him. You might as well get used to the idea.'

'But I'm not——' began Lisa hotly and then broke off.

Matt gazed at her steadily and a flush spread over her face. She swallowed hard and tried again.

'But I'm not sure it's the right thing to do just at the moment,' she muttered, avoiding his gaze. 'I'd really rather go back to Melbourne as soon as possible.'

The silence between them lengthened. Lisa felt as if she was under the glare of a police search light and she didn't dare raise her eyes, because she knew she couldn't sustain the deception any longer if she did. She would simply blurt out the truth. And she didn't want to see the incredulity and contempt in Matt's face when he learned how she had lied to him and taken advantage of his hospitality. Crazy though it might be, she wanted his good opinion. When his warm fingers touched her chin and raised it, she flinched.

'Look at me,' he ordered.

She darted him a furtive, anxious glance and looked hastily away again.

'Why don't you want to stay?' he demanded.

'I can't,' she said hoarsely.

'Why not?'

She bit her lip and remained silent.

'Is it because I kissed you two nights ago and you responded?'

Lisa's eyes widened in alarm, but she still said nothing. Matt held her shoulders and looked down at her. She was tall, but he was taller still. Tingling thrills of warmth coursed through her at his touch and she wanted to burrow into his arms and beg him to hold her, but there was too much standing in their way. Tim. This crazy deception. Andrea. Yes! Andrea. She must keep that in mind to give her the strength to resist him.

'I'd rather forget that ever happened,' she said stiffly.

Matt's face hardened and abruptly he released her.

'Then we will,' he said with a shrug. 'I won't force myself on you, Lisa, you can trust me for that. Just tell me the truth about what you want.'

Her heart began to beat in a slow, unsteady rhythm and she stared at him with a stricken expression. What she wanted was him, but she could hardly tell him that. She didn't even want to admit it to herself. Suddenly with a muffled gasp she broke away and walked across the room.

'All I want is to go back to Melbourne,' she said over her shoulder. 'Now. As soon as possible.'

The silence was unbearable, suffocating, broken only by the sound of Matt's deep, slow, tranquil breathing and the tick of a clock in the hall. At last he spoke.

'You say you want to leave. Does this mean you're not going to marry Tim?'

Lisa's eyes flashed. This was all Tim's fault and, as usual, he had skipped out and left her to deal with the consequences of his crazy scheme.

'Why don't you ask him about that?' she burst out.

'I might, if I knew where he was. I tried phoning him this morning in Melbourne without any success. Do you know where he is?'

Lisa's eyes met his and then darted hastily away. No, she didn't know for sure where Tim was, but she could make a pretty fair guess. Barbara's parents had a beach house down on the Victorian coast at Portsea where she and Tim often fled on weekends. It wouldn't surprise her if they were there right now, but she felt in no mood to cooperate with Matt.

'No,' she said bluntly.

He frowned.

'Well, in that case I can only ask you for the information I want. Are you going to marry him?'

'I will if I want to,' she replied defiantly. 'You can't stop me!'

He smiled at that, a smile that sent tremors of uneasiness right down her spine.

'No? We'll have to see, won't we?'

His air of calm amusement infuriated her.

'You think you're clever, don't you?' she demanded. 'Well, you certainly can't make me stay here on the farm against my own will. No doubt, if you're half as smart as you think you are, you'll soon succeed in tracking down Tim. But I'm leaving. I'll take a taxi if necessary.'

He was still unruffled, still calm, amused and wholly in control of the situation.

'There's no need to be melodramatic,' he said. 'I'll drive you to the airport tomorrow morning, if that's what you want.'

'It is.'

'There's just one more thing, Lisa.'

His hand touched her arm. It was a completely harmless, friendly gesture, but it sent tingles of alarm and excitement coursing through her.

'Yes?'

'If you do have any suspicions as to where Tim is,' he said, choosing his words slowly and deliberately, 'then for heaven's sake ask him to contact me. Quite apart from any ideas he might have about marrying you, it's high time that Tim and I had a long talk about his plans for the future. I'm not an unreasonable man. I'll try to listen fairly to anything he has to say to me. Will you tell him that? If you know where he is.'

She dropped her eyes, unable to meet his gaze.

'I'll try,' she muttered at last.

He still did not release his grip on her arm. She could feel the warmth of his fingers through her blouse and wondered half hysterically if he could feel the way her pulse was speeding up or hear the shallow, uneven rhythm of her breathing.

'Good,' he added tranquilly. 'Oh, and there's something else. I'm planning to drive up to Hobart later today, because one of my tuna fishing vessels is being repaired at a boat yard there and I need to check on it. I thought I might have dinner and see a show at the casino afterwards. I'd be very pleased if you'd join me.'

She glanced at him with a tormented expression. What was he after? More information about Tim or...something else? She simply couldn't tell. The expression in his blue eyes was completely unfathomable, but it panicked her, just the same. She heard her voice coming out, high and nervous.

'I don't think I——'

'There's no pressure,' he assured her, releasing her arm and giving her a brief, wry smile. 'But I'd like you to come.'

She stared at him suspiciously and opened her mouth to say no, but the words stuck in her throat.

'Well?' he prompted.

'Yes,' she croaked.

Lying on her bed ten minutes later with the door firmly shut, Lisa wondered bitterly whether there was any hereditary insanity in her family. Why on earth had she agreed to go out to dinner with Matt, who was as dangerous as a nuclear warhead? Oh, stop fussing about it, Lisa, she told herself crossly. It's only dinner. He's hardly going to fling you on your back in the middle of the table and ravish you in the revolving restaurant. Yet the mere thought of that, outrageous as it was, sent an unfamiliar, pulsating warmth throbbing through her entire body. For a moment she revelled in the fantasy. It was madness, pure madness. But how wonderful it would be if Matt could evict all the other diners and staff, lock the doors and take her passionately right there in the restaurant. She could almost hear the clatter of silverware, smell the fiery, intoxicating aroma of an overturned brandy balloon, feel the warmth of candle-light flickering near her naked skin. And Matt . . . how would Matt look and feel? Her tongue slid between her teeth as she remembered the warmth of his kisses, the salty taste of his skin, the hard, rippling potency of his muscles as he had crushed her against him on that un-forgettable evening only two days ago. Those kisses had left her aching and unfulfilled, but she knew instinc-tively that if he ever took their lovemaking to its natural conclusion, she would experience an abandonment she had only dreamt of so far. She wanted him, wanted him with a violence and urgency that shocked her. How can I possibly be thinking these things? she wondered in dismay. I came up to my room to calm down and instead I'm having crazy fantasies about him. The trouble is that I only have to look at Matt Lansdon and I feel as if my whole body is turning to molten fire. Oh, why did Tim ever get me into this mess?

The thought of Tim was like a dash of cold water. She sat up and glared at her reflection in the cheval mirror at the foot of the bed. Why should Tim get off scot-free? He was the one who had caused all this trouble, wasn't he? Well, why shouldn't he cop some of the fallout? Why should Lisa be the only one to suffer? Surely there must be something she could do about it.... Suddenly a wicked gleam sparkled in her eyes and she picked up the telephone next to the bed and dialled the number of his girlfriend's beach house.

'Barbara? This is Lisa. Hi, how are you? Is Tim there?... Sorry, I don't believe you. Look, just tell him this, will you? If he is there, he's got ten seconds to get on the phone to me now, or I'm spilling the beans to his uncle about everything. The painting lessons, cutting classes from accountancy, the true story about marrying me... Oh, didn't he tell you about that, Barb?... Sure, go ahead, beat him over the head with a frying pan and give him one for me while you're at it. But I really do need to talk to him.'

At the other end of the line there was the sound of upraised voices, followed by a slamming door. Then Tim came on the line, sounding aggrieved.

'Why did you tell Barbara that garbage about me being engaged to you?' he demanded resentfully. 'You're such a dork sometimes, Lisa! Now she's gone off in a huff. What do you want, anyway?'

'I want you, Timothy,' cooed Lisa. 'I want you to get your cute little self down here to Tasmania right now. Tomorrow at the latest.'

Tim gave a muffled snort of laughter.

'You must be kidding!'

'No, I'm not,' she said with a flash of annoyance. 'Now you listen to me, Tim, because I mean this. You're going to come back here and deal with your power-crazed uncle yourself. Or else I'm going to tell him the complete truth about our intended marriage.'

'The complete truth?' echoed Tim in horror. 'He'd murder me, Lisa. He'd string me up by my little toes for making such a fool of him.'

'See if I care. Either you arrive tomorrow on the first plane or I'll blow the whistle on you!'

Tim groaned. 'You wouldn't! Oh, Lisa, have a heart!'

'I do have a heart,' she said sweetly. 'And it's made of stone. Are you coming, Tim, or do I spill the beans?'

'He'll cut off my allowance if you tell him the truth,' protested Tim. 'He'll exterminate both of us. Slowly.'

Lisa grinned gleefully, enjoying the intoxicating sense of power that was rising inside her like floodwaters.

'So what?' she challenged. 'I'm not related to him. I can leave whenever I want. It's a pity you can't, isn't it, Tim?'

'Lisa,' said Tim bitterly. 'You know how you gave me those silk pyjamas for my birthday two months ago and I told you that you were a really warm-hearted person? Well, I take that back!'

'Oh, stop blubbering, Tim. I hate to hear an almost grown man cry. Now are you coming back or not?'

'Yes. Damn you. Yes! I'll be on the morning plane tomorrow so for pity's sake keep your lips zipped until then.'

There was a crash at the other end of the line. Lisa chuckled softly as she set down the receiver. Poor Tim! She didn't like his chances of keeping his secret for long once he was in Matt's presence, but deep down she felt that the best thing he could do was to confide in his uncle, even if a row resulted. In any case it was not her worry any more. She would be leaving tomorrow. An odd pang of regret shot through her at the thought and she rose to her feet and padded across to the mirror. What had Matt said about her? 'You have vitality, gusto, humour and blatant sex appeal.' She smiled bleakly. He should have added a complete lack of scruples and a vast capacity for deceit to the list! Would Matt despise her when he finally discovered their deception? Oh, what did it matter anyway? He already thought she was a gold-digger, so he might as well realise that she was a liar into the bargain. Yet an indefinable yearning fluttered deep inside her as she dressed in a flowing russet silk slacks suit and fastened a gold and pearl necklace around her throat. I wish, she thought. I wish... She sighed and left the thought unfinished.

The wistful mood clung to her throughout the two-hour drive to Hobart, so that she returned only absent-minded replies to Matt's attempts at conversation. At last he flashed her a thoughtful look and thrust a cas-sette into the small player in the dashboard. *Carmen*. As Bizet's glorious music swirled around them in a flood of sound, Lisa found to her horror that her throat felt tight and painful and her eyes were prickling. She blinked twice and glared out the window. I'm not falling in love with him, she told herself savagely. I'm not! I couldn't be such a fool....

It was another ten kilometres before she felt calm enough to look at him. He was gazing at the road ahead with total absorption, lost in his thoughts, so that she was able to scrutinize him without embarrassment. Hungrily she took in every detail about him—the way his dark hair waved vigorously back from his tanned forehead, the few threads of silver at his temple, the keen, almost scowling gaze of his blue eyes under the thick, dark brows, the twitch of a muscle in his cheek as he gritted his teeth. As usual he was conservatively dressed, but even his clothes held an unexpected fascination for Lisa.

Men didn't wear fashionable charcoal-grey Italian suits and crisp white shirts and red silk ties and glossy handmade leather shoes unless they were achievers. Not that Matt seemed to care a damn about fashion. He simply wore the kind of clothes that had the stamp of money and sophistication as carelessly as if they were cast-off jeans and old T-shirts. His naturally fastidious nature wouldn't allow him to appear in scuffed shoes or a crumpled jacket. Beyond that, Lisa doubted whether he thought twice about what he was wearing. It probably never occurred to him that his clothes, like everything else about him, projected an aura of breeding and good taste and old money. All the things Lisa had once thought were as out of date as dinosaurs. So why did she get this perverse thrill of pride and pleasure at seeing Matt beside her, looking so self-assured, so smugly arrogant, so certain of his place in the universe? It baffled her. For the first time in her life she felt small, fragile, deliciously feminine, overpowered by the uncompromising masculinity of the man who accompanied her. And the awful thing was that she loved every moment of it. You'd better watch out, Lisa! she warned herself silently. Matt Lansdon is conservative, traditional and narrow-minded. He's not the right kind of man for you. And even if he was, there's no way he'd ever marry an artist. She almost gasped as the full significance of her thoughts dawned on her. Who said anything about marriage, anyway? she told herself fiercely.

By the time the golden grass and tree-clad hills gave way to straggling suburbs, and the wide, blue expanse of the Derwent River came into view, Lisa felt like a nervous wreck. It was exhausting talking to yourself. It was even worse sitting in the confined interior of a car with a man who emanated sex appeal like some toxic, nuclear radiation. She wished passionately that she had simply stayed at the farm, but she could not help feeling a treacherous thrill of pleasure when Matt opened the car door in the boat yard car park and stood gazing down at her with a faint smile.

'Come and see my boat,' he invited.

She followed him down the sloping path that led to the slip yard and tried to keep her mind on tuna fishing. It wasn't easy. The estuary spread out before her like a lake of beaten gold in the glow of the setting sun. The warm, clovelike scent of stocks rose from the garden of a whitewashed Georgian cottage overlooking the slip yard, and the air echoed with interesting sounds. The wire stays of moored yachts clanging against the masts ·in a sudden puff of sea breeze, waves slapping on the rocks, seagulls shrieking, the sound of a dog barking in a back garden, a mother calling her children in to tea. Lisa paused at the top of the bank and looked at Matt, standing silhouetted against the white hull of the fishing boat on the slips. In that moment a pang of longing as sharp as a physical pain pierced her. I love him, she thought. I want to stay here and be part of all this with him. I want him to claim me as his woman, his wife, the mother of his children. Oh, heavens, what a fool I am!

'Lisa? Are you coming down?'

With a small shudder she regained her composure and picked her way down the bank to join him. He introduced her to the boat builder and, to cover her embarrassment, Lisa asked a lot of babbling questions.

'Have you been involved in tuna fishing long? What's wrong with the boat? Did anyone get hurt when it was damaged? Is tuna fishing dangerous?'

Matt frowned slightly, as if perplexed about why she wouldn't meet his eyes. And no wonder, thought Lisa irritably. I must look like a total moron glancing up at him every ten seconds and blushing like a tomato when he looks at me.

'I've owned boats in the Pirates Bay fleet for thirteen years now,' Matt replied evenly. 'This one dragged its anchor and ran aground on rocks. The bow was holed, but luckily nobody was hurt. Of course, the sea can always be very cruel and dangerous. My cousin Graham was lost overboard in heavy weather several years ago. It hit us all pretty hard.'

His gaze took on a grim, distant quality, then he shrugged suddenly with the ghost of a smile.

'Well, there's no point being morbid,' he said. Turning to the boat builder, he shook hands with him. 'Thanks, Russell. You've done a great job in a very short time. I appreciate the speed.'

'No worries, mate. You've always been a real good bloke to deal with, so I reckon I owe you something. Nice meeting you, Lisa.'

As she followed Matt to the car, Lisa sucked thoughtfully on her lower lip. However much she might try to tell herself that Tim's uncle was an ogre, she knew deep down that it wasn't true. Matt had seemed genuinely distressed by his cousin's death, even though it had happened several years ago. And, what was more, that boat builder had obviously felt a deep respect and liking for him. It just didn't fit with the image she had of a man who was overbearing, hard to get along with and indifferent to other people's feelings. Then the memory of Andrea flashed into her mind and she felt deeply confused. What was the truth about Matt Lansdon? Was he reliable and worthy of trust, or callous and exploitative? Lisa was still wondering as they arrived in the Asian restaurant at the casino.

By now the sun had set, although a pale green twilight was lingering around the hills on the opposite shore. The restaurant lights were deliberately kept low, in order not to detract from the panorama outside. The flickering table lamps gave the room an atmosphere of mystery that fascinated Lisa, so that her head swivelled as the maître d'hôtel showed them to one of the best tables overlooking the water. He summoned a waiter to take their orders for drinks and then withdrew.

'What an amazing place!' exclaimed Lisa as she looked at the Chinese screens and hanging lanterns that adorned the room. 'You would almost believe we were in Hong Kong.'

'You wouldn't get such an uninterrupted view in Hong Kong!' said Matt with a chuckle as he leaned comfortably back in his chair. 'Too many skyscrapers in front of the harbour.'

'You sound as if you've been there,' said Lisa.

He shrugged. 'I spent three years there.'

'Really?' she asked with interest. 'What were you doing?'

'A business venture. My farm and fishing fleet in Tasmania were under control and I was bored, so I thought I'd open a factory in Hong Kong manufacturing small computer components.'

Lisa's mouth fell open.

'You're amazing,' she said frankly. 'Not a bit like the way Tim described you. So, tell me, what was it like living in Hong Kong?'

'Exciting,' replied Matt. 'It's a pity you weren't there with me. You would have loved it, especially since you enjoy exotic food.'

It's a pity you weren't there with me. The words echoed in Lisa's ears. There was a tantalizing hint of intimacy about them, but Matt didn't give her time to linger over his meaning.

'Still, I'm sure we can find something exotic for you to eat here tonight,' he continued. 'I'd like to make it an evening for you to remember.'

It was certainly that. In fact it was magical. As they worked their way through spring rolls, crab meat soup, Peking duck, braised vegetables and other delights, Lisa realized that she had far more in common with Matt than she had ever dreamed possible. Not only was he knowledgeable about art and opera, but he had travelled in every part of the globe that she had ever visited and far more besides. Tim's sarcastic dismissal of his uncle as a grumpy old grazier was obviously light-years away from the truth. There was no doubt that Matt Lansdon could ride a horse and muster cattle and mend fences, but there was far more to him than that. So much more that when Lisa found herself waltzing slowly around the ballroom floor clasped against him just before midnight, she knew that she was falling dizzily, hopelessly in love with him. But the most memorable moment of all came when they returned to the farm and Matt helped her out of the car and stood looking gravely down at her in the moonlight. Lisa's heart fluttered wildly as he took a step closer. Almost as if he didn't trust himself to touch her, he clenched his hands at his sides.

'I wish you'd change your mind and stay on, Lisa,' he said harshly. 'Will you think about it?'

She opened her mouth to speak, but her throat felt dry and tight.

'Yes,' she whispered at last.

She did think about it. In fact she thought about it all night, so that she was quite unable to sleep for the turbulent sense of exhilaration and apprehension that gripped her. Obviously she had been quite wrong in her assessment of Matt. In the beginning she had thought he was ruthless and calculating and she had felt quite certain that he disapproved of her. Well, now she felt equally certain that she had misjudged him. Even if Matt had been genuinely suspicious of her at first, he had obviously changed his mind. He had had the courage to start afresh and reveal his growing regard for her quite openly. Shouldn't she be equally brave? Yet before she and Matt could have an honest relationship of any kind, there was one major hurdle she would have to clear. Shortly after dawn she took a hard decision. She would tell Matt the whole truth about herself and Tim and the deception they had practised on him. If Matt still wanted her to stay on after that, she would.

She could hear him moving about in his study downstairs and, feeling as if she was about to confess to murder, she pulled on her dressing gown and slippers and tiptoed down to find him. As she approached the room, she heard the sound of his upraised voice and paused for a moment in bewilderment. Then she realized that he was talking on the telephone. She hesitated, uncertain whether to knock or go away. As she turned to leave, she overheard something that made her blood chill in her veins.

'Don't be ridiculous, Andrea,' exclaimed Matt in exasperation. 'You've got to stop clinging to me and make a life of your own. It's the best thing for you and Justin... No! Of course I'm not falling in love with Lisa. If you want to know the truth, it's Tim who wants to marry her. I'm just deliberately leading her on, so I can show him how fickle she really is.'

CHAPTER FIVE

FOR a moment Lisa was so stunned that she felt nothing. Then a burning wave of anger, embarrassment and humiliation swept over her as the full sting of Matt's words hit home. The swine! He hadn't simply been attracted to her against his better judgment, he hadn't even been making a straightforward attempt to seduce her openly. Instead he had been deliberately leading her on with a subtlety that was all the more cruel for being so effective. To think that she had believed his reluctance to touch her was motivated by a sense of decency! And instead it was just a deceitful trick to gain her trust so that he could make a fool of her more effectively! He had admitted as much to Andrea. The thought of Andrea made her wince. She felt almost equally indignant on the other woman's behalf as she did on her own. For a moment she was tempted to storm into the study, slap Matt Lansdon's face and tell him exactly what she thought of him. But that wouldn't solve anything and it would only make her look even more ridiculous.

Controlling herself with an effort, she tiptoed upstairs and sat in her room, seething helplessly for half an hour until inspiration slowly began to take shape in the back of her mind. What she wanted was revenge. Well, why not turn Matt's weapon back on him? He had planned to lead her on and make her fall in love with him and then humiliate her, hadn't he? Fine! Then she would do exactly the same thing to him. Of course, it would mean that she couldn't go back to Melbourne just yet. And she would need Tim's help....

Matt was sitting at the dining table when she arrived downstairs for breakfast. He looked as well-groomed and suave as ever, with his dark, shining hair, his blue and white Pierre Cardin shirt and his crisp beige slacks. As Lisa entered the room he looked up and smiled at her. If she hadn't overheard his vile conversation with Andrea a short time earlier, Lisa would have been attracted by that smile. It was exactly right for the occasion. A wry, quizzical twist of the lips with only the faintest lurking hint of sensuality. Not enough to frighten her off, oh, no, Matt Lansdon was too clever for that! Just enough to intrigue and flatter her. Remembering how he had held back from kissing her the previous evening as if he had had to struggle with his feelings, Lisa almost ground her teeth in rage. Instead she summoned enough self-control to give him exactly the same kind of smile in return. Rueful, lingering, with a touch of regret and tempestuous desire.

'I hope I haven't kept you waiting,' she said in a soft, breathy voice. 'But I promise I'll eat my breakfast quickly. I've already got my bags packed for the trip home.'

'You're really leaving then?' There was no mistaking the tinge of surprise and annoyance in his voice.

'Yes.'

Lisa had thought carefully about the matter and decided her decision to stay would have far more impact if she made it at the airport rather than at the farm. Besides, that would give her the pleasure of inflicting an unnecessary hour and a half of driving each way on Matt. What was more, it had the added advantage they should be able to bring Tim home with them from the airport.

If she was going to lure Matt into her nets like a nineteen thirties vamp, she had the nervous feeling that some kind of chaperon might make her feel safer. This game could turn out to be highly dangerous.

'I'm sorry to hear that,' said Matt huskily. He passed her the toast rack and his fingers brushed against hers so lightly that it might have been an accident. 'Are you sure you won't change your mind?'

'Quite sure,' murmured Lisa with a deliberate touch of hesitation in her voice.

Their eyes met and it was like the clash of two fencing swords locking in unyielding antagonism. Lisa felt a thrill that was part rage and part aching, sexual desire throb through her at that contact. Matt Lansdon might be the most unscrupulous swine alive, but oh, Lord, he was irresistible! When he looked at her with that smoky, devouring need she felt breathless and disoriented. For one petrified moment she thought he was going to seize her wrist, haul her across the table and take her then and there. If he did, she doubted whether she would have the strength or sanity to resist. Instead, he simply rose to his feet and fetched a silver chafing dish from the sideboard. She swallowed and dropped her gaze, feeling slightly dizzy.

'Just tell me if your plans change,' he said.

Afterwards she could hardly remember what she had eaten. Bacon definitely. Crisp, fragrant curls of it. Fried egg? Tomato? She wasn't sure. All she could remember was the shape of Matt's lean brown hands holding out the dish to her with the dark hair straggling over the backs of his wrists and the indefinably threatening but enticing way that his blue eyes narrowed as he looked at her...why did he disturb her so much?

It was still very early when they sped up the highway through dew-spangled paddocks and coils of morning mist towards the airport. When they arrived, Matt took charge of her bags and ticket.

'Let me handle the check-in for you,' he offered blandly. 'It's always deadly boring. Go and have a cup of coffee and I'll get you when it's organized.'

Something about the glint in his eyes warned her this time and she wasn't in the least surprised when he joined her ten minutes later with bad news.

'I'm awfully sorry about this, Lisa, but there seems to be some kind of mix-up. They haven't got your name down for this flight and it's fully booked. I can't imagine what's happened.'

I bet you can't, thought Lisa sourly. But I can. I wonder how much it cost you to organize this? Since she had no intention of catching the flight anyway, she wasn't genuinely upset, but she felt she ought to put on a good show.

'What a shame!' she exclaimed. 'Oh, Matt. And you promised you'd phone yesterday and confirm the booking. I thought everything you did was always so efficient.'

He frowned at this criticism.

'Well, these things happen,' he said with a touch of irritation. 'There's not much point waiting around for nothing, though, is there? I've already put your bags in the car, so shall we go back to the farm?'

'Oh, not yet!' pleaded Lisa, who was beginning to enjoy herself. 'At least let's wait till the plane arrives from Melbourne and takes off again. You never know, there may be a cancellation that I can get. Or Tim may be on the incoming flight.'

Matt gave a low growl of laughter. 'I hardly think so. You ought to face facts, my love. Tim's deserted you.'

'Oh, I'm sure you're wrong,' cooed Lisa. 'As a matter of fact, I have the strangest hunch that Tim's going to be on that very plane.'

Matt scowled. 'What do you mean?' he asked suspiciously. 'You're scheming something, aren't you?'

'Me?' replied Lisa in a deadpan voice. 'Of course not! I'm no more capable of scheming than you are, Matt.'

She couldn't help being gratified by the thunderous expression on Matt's face a few minutes later as Tim emerged on the front stairs of the plane from Melbourne. While his nephew was still striding across the tarmac, Matt glowered at Lisa.

'You set this up, didn't you?' he asked angrily. 'You knew he was coming?'

'Oh, no. It was just feminine instinct. You know, when a woman's planning to marry, she gets a mysterious sense of closeness to her lover. Almost like a psychic bond that——'

'I could wring your mysterious little neck!' snapped Matt. 'And kindly don't remind me that Tim is your lover. You needn't think there will be any of that going on under my roof.'

Lisa smirked at him infuriatingly.

'Don't worry, Matt, we'll be discreet,' she promised. 'Wasn't it a shame that there wasn't a seat available for me on the plane? If you were trying to keep us apart, it would have been so much easier if I had been flying off to Melbourne in a moment. As it is, I'll just have to stay with dear Tim, won't I?'

At that moment 'dear Tim' arrived to find his uncle and his flatmate quarrelling in heated undertones. He looked more alarmed than delighted when Lisa swept him into a rapturous hug and kissed him effusively. His uncle's greeting was limited to a surly grunt, after which he strode off to look for Tim's incoming luggage.

'I suppose you brought that awful old backpack with you again?' he snarled over his shoulder.

'Yeah, thanks, Unc.'

'And don't call me Unc!'

'What's the matter with him? You haven't told him the truth about our dodgy marriage, have you, Lisa? Or about my art studies?'

'No. We're having a cold war. Or a raging hot war, more like it. I'll tell you all about it later. Now, what about you? Is everything okay?'

Tim's face lit up.

'Everything's bloody marvellous,' he agreed. 'Lisa, guess what? When I got home from Barb's place yesterday, I found there was a letter waiting for me. I've been short-listed for the Buller Art Prize. I'm one of four finalists!'

Lisa gasped. 'You're joking?'

'No, it's the truth. I'll get three years studying art in Paris if I win. The only trouble is that they want us to do another painting each as a tie breaker before the New Year. I want to finish *Female Nude on a Spring Afternoon* if I possibly can. Lisa, you've got to help me!'

Lisa looked uneasy. What kind of help did he mean? Did he mean posing nude? For some complicated reason that was obscurely connected with Matt, she no longer felt comfortable about the idea of doing that. But of course, if Tim only wanted technical advice....

'Sure,' she agreed warmly. 'Look, Matt's coming back. Why don't you tell him about this? If anything could convince him that you ought to be studying art, this will.'

Tim shook his head stubbornly.

'No. I'll tell him if I win the prize, but not before. It will only lead to a row and I won't be able to paint well if I'm all churned up. Listen, what are you and Matt fighting about?'

It was a question that Lisa couldn't answer for quite a long time. During the drive to the farm, Matt was in a foul mood and the need for secrecy limited her conversation with Tim drastically. At last, on the pretext of carrying Lisa's bags upstairs, Tim ensconced himself comfortably in her room and lay on her bed, flexing his biceps and admiring them, while Lisa unpacked her clothes again. After an hour of telling her about the Buller Prize, he finally exhausted the fascinating subject of himself and was ready to talk about her.

'So what are you and Matt fighting about?' he repeated.

'He's a hard-hearted, insensitive, scheming brute!' burst out Lisa.

'Told you,' agreed Tim smugly, tossing a segment of orange into the air and trying to catch it in his open mouth. It landed on the chain-stitched quilt, leaving an ugly stain. 'What's he done?'

'You're disgusting,' complained Lisa, fetching a damp cotton ball from the bathroom and attacking the stain. 'I'll tell you what he's done, he's humiliated me.'

'How?'

'Well, he took me out to dinner and made up to me, but so subtly that I was really taken in. I feel such a fool! I was honestly starting to think he was completely sincere. Then this morning I overheard him on the telephone telling someone that he was deliberately leading me on, just so that he could show you how fickle I was.'

Tim whistled and sat up. 'That's a bit rough,' he exclaimed. 'It's not as though you've ever been the tarty sort. Do you want me to tell him that?'

'No! I don't care what he thinks about me.'

Tim rolled his eyes sceptically. 'Who did he say this to anyway?'

Lisa hesitated and brought out the name with difficulty.

'Andrea Spencer. Do you know her?'

The shock in Tim's face told her unmistakably that he did, but he shrugged uneasily and his gaze flicked away.

'Not really.'

'You do! What do you know about her? Tell me!'

Tim's eyes tracked reluctantly back to hers.

'Only that she has a kid who is the spitting image of Matt,' he admitted. 'Everyone says that it's his, but he won't marry her.'

Once when she was eleven years old, Lisa had fallen off a horse and broken a rib. Now she felt the same sense of pain and disbelief. A shocked, wounded feeling that pierced her when she breathed.

'It might be just gossip!' she flared.

'It might be. But this is a small place and it seems likely enough. Women have always chased after Matt in droves, you know.'

'And you really think he'd be mean enough to get a woman pregnant and refuse to marry her?'

Tim looked uncomfortable.

'No, I wouldn't have thought so,' he said frankly. 'But it sure looks that way, doesn't it?'

'Yes, it does.' To Lisa's horror, she could not keep a faint tremor out of her voice.

'You've fallen for him, haven't you?' demanded Tim. 'It's only three miserable days since you met him and you've already fallen for him.'

'I haven't! I hate him.'

'Well, why should you care whether he fathered Andrea's child or not?'

'I don't!' cried Lisa.

Tim looked sceptical. 'Don't give me that. It's written all over you. You fancy him just as much as he fancies you.'

'I don't! Anyway, what makes you think he fancies me?'

'The way he behaved all the way back from the airport today,' said Tim slyly. 'He didn't want me there one little bit. He was just eating you up with his eyes. I'll bet if I hadn't been in the back seat he would have pulled off the road near some quiet little beach and started ripping your clothes off.'

'Don't be stupid!' cried Lisa, suppressing a treacherous twinge of excitement at the thought. 'Get this through your thick head, will you, Tim? I certainly don't intend to let Matt seduce me and I don't suppose he has any genuine interest in doing so. The only reason he pretended he did was so that he could hurt and humiliate me and I'll never forgive him for it.'

'So I suppose you're going to turn wimpy and run off to Melbourne because you're so upset about it,' said Tim in disgust. 'Just when I need you to help me finish my painting.'

'No, I'm not going to Melbourne.'

'Then what are you going to do?'

'I'm going to pay him back for treating me so badly.'

A faint gleam of interest dawned in Tim's face. 'How?'

'Well, two can play at his rotten little game. I'm going to do exactly the same thing he tried to do to me. I'll lead him on and then let him know that it was all just a spiteful trick. Let's see how he likes it.'

Tim gave an explosive chuckle.

'That should be worth watching,' he conceded. 'But you'll have to mind that you don't really fall in love with him.'

'Never!' vowed Lisa.

'So what exactly are you planning to do?' asked Tim.

'Well,' said Lisa thoughtfully. 'It's best if he thinks it's happening gradually. I'm going to act as if I'm really planning to marry you at first, but let him think that I can't help being attracted to him, as well. I'll lure him in and once he's made a complete fool out of himself, I'll tell him the truth, that the whole thing's just a game to pay him back.'

Tim winced. 'I almost feel sorry for him,' he said.

'Well, don't be! He doesn't deserve your sympathy.'

'That's true. And if you stay here, you'll be able to advise me on my painting technique, won't you? And help stop Uncle Matt from finding out that I'm working on the painting?'

'That's crazy, Tim. I don't mind advising you, but how can you prevent Matt from finding out what you're doing? He's bound to realize the truth.'

'No, he's not,' insisted Tim. His gaze travelled across to the painting, which was propped against Lisa's bedroom wall in a protective box. 'He's already swallowed my story that it's just one of your pieces that I brought over from Melbourne for you.'

'I know,' said Lisa ironically. 'But once you get out your brushes and paints and stand there daubing the canvas, don't you think he might figure out that you're the one who's working on it?'

Tim shook his head.

'No, I've got an idea. Have you seen that little cottage over the next hill? The one that used to have a tenant farmer, but is deserted now? I'm going to move in there and use it as a studio. You can come and visit me and we'll let Matt think it's a love nest where we do unspeakable things together....'

Tim made a graphic gesture with his right hand and gave Lisa a leering wink. She choked with laughter and collapsed on the bed beside him.

'Tim, you are utterly evil!' she exclaimed.

'I know, I take after my uncle. But it's a perfect scheme, isn't it? He'll be really browned off about the pair of us vanishing there, but I'm sure he won't actually stoop to spying on us. And once he starts to get really jealous, you can drop a few hints that you might prefer him to me. What do you think?'

Lisa felt a brief pang of conscience, but thrust it aside. Matt deserved this!

'I love it!' she said firmly and flung her arms around Tim in a gigantic bear hug.

At that moment there was a perfunctory knock at the door and Matt strode in. He stopped dead at the sight of them sprawled on the bed together, and a shadow like a thundercloud crossed his face. The rage and jealousy that emanated from him was so intense that Lisa felt her heart give a lurch of alarm. Then Matt advanced towards them, his eyes narrowed and his mouth set in a grim line. He gritted his teeth as he stood glaring down at them, and for one horrified moment Lisa thought violence was going to erupt. While her heart was still hammering in her chest, Matt suddenly lunged forward and seized his nephew by the front of his shirt. Lifting the horrified Tim bodily into the air, he set him down on the carpet.

'You! Downstairs. At once. I need you outside mustering stock. As for you, Lisa Hayward, I've warned you once already. I won't have that kind of outrageous behaviour practised under my roof between a grown woman and someone who is no more than a feckless boy. Whatever the legalities of the situation, I am the master in this house and you will obey my rules while you stay here. Do I make myself clear?'

Lisa flinched, caught between a hysterical urge to burst out laughing and an equally hysterical urge to fling herself into Matt's arms and lift her lips to his. Defiantly she wondered how long his opposition to her outrageous behaviour would last if she did. Fortunately some remaining shred of sanity held her back. Her eyes dropped before his stern, implacable gaze.

'Yes,' she muttered and had to stop herself from adding, 'sir.'

'Good. Then kindly occupy yourself in some more respectable fashion for the rest of the day. I'll see you at dinner.'

Dinner was over an hour late that evening since the two Lansdons had stayed out working till darkness fell and then had to bathe and change. Matt arrived at the table looking fresh and fit with his damp hair slicked back and the hint of a smile curling his lower lip, but Tim was clearly exhausted. There was a sticking plaster on his left hand and he almost fell asleep over the mushroom soup. When Matt vanished into the kitchen to fetch the beef casserole and braised vegetables, Lisa looked sympathetically at Tim.

'Are you all right?' she whispered.

Tim opened his eyes.

'No, I'm knackered,' he complained bitterly. 'Matt thinks everyone can last sixteen hours on a horse the way he can, but I hate it. I've cut my bloody hand on the fencing wire and you ought to see my saddle sores.'

'I don't think that would be a good idea right now,' said Lisa hastily.

'Well, maybe not, but I've had it,' grumbled Tim. 'I'm warning you, Lisa, I've got to think of some way of getting out of this. I'll never get my painting finished if I don't.'

'Poor Tim. Don't worry, I'll help you in any way I can.'

She wished she hadn't said that when Tim flashed his angelic smile at her the following morning at breakfast, gazed from her to Matt and back again and then spoke.

'I've got a great idea,' he announced. 'Lisa's been dying to do some landscape paintings, Uncle Matt, so why don't I take her over to our fishing cabin at Fortescue Bay and let her paint for a week or so?'

Matt gave his nephew a glinting look.

'I've got a better idea,' he said in a hard voice. 'You can stay here and get some more practical experience on the farm, Tim, and I'll take Lisa to the cabin.'

Tim could scarcely contain his triumph and Lisa her indignation as Matt took the dirty plates out to the kitchen.

'You worm,' she said, once he was safely out of earshot. 'You low-down, treacherous worm! I don't want to spend a week in a cabin with Matt.'

Tim grinned and poured himself fresh coffee.

'It'll give you a great chance to let him think you're falling for him,' he pointed out unrepentantly.

'Oh, yes? And what if it gives him a great chance to....'

'Force you into bed with him? Oh, come on, Lisa. Matt's never had to force anyone. I'm sure Andrea dropped into his arms like a ripe little plum. He won't try anything unless he thinks you're willing.'

'How comforting,' said Lisa coldly.

'Come on, Lisa, be a sport. I need time to finish my painting. Promise you'll do this for me.'

Lisa sighed. That argument, at least, was unanswerable.

'I hate you, Tim,' she muttered. 'All right, I'll do it.'

They set off shortly after breakfast the following morning. It was a warm day but Lisa felt clammy with apprehension as she climbed into the passenger seat of the four-wheel drive vehicle and shot Matt an uneasy glance. Was she insane to have agreed to this? The prospect of a week alone with him filled her with as much dread as the idea of spending a week in a cage with a hungry lion. She gritted her teeth, feeling impatient with her own misgivings. She ought to be pleased! This trip would give her plenty of time to make the opening moves in her nerve-racking game of revenge. She knew there was a good chance she could make Matt believe she was passionately attracted to him, that she was rapidly becoming a victim to his raw, sensual appeal. The only risk was that she might begin to believe it herself. Lisa flinched at the thought and unconsciously drew herself an inch or two farther away from him.

'Is something wrong?' he asked pleasantly.

'N-no, nothing,' she stammered.

'That's a relief. You looked rather alarmed, although I can't imagine why. After all, this is meant to be a pleasure trip, isn't it? A week's fishing for me, a week's painting for you. And a chance to get to know each other. There isn't any hidden agenda, is there?'

'No,' choked Lisa, and felt a fiery wave of colour rush through her neck and face. 'I don't know what you mean.'

'Don't you?' His voice was cool, mocking, amused and, although she refused to look up and meet his eyes, she had the uneasy sensation that they were boring right through her. 'That's good, because I had the oddest feeling when Tim came out to say goodbye that you and he were scheming together. I wouldn't do that if I were you, Lisa. You might regret it.'

A shudder went through her as he started up the engine and turned the vehicle down the driveway. Who was playing games with whom? she wondered bitterly as they bumped down the rough, gravel road. Yet her apprehension gradually receded in the pleasure of the journey. The sun was beating down out of the cloudless blue sky, the jade green sea was roaring on the beaches, cattle stood knee high in the long grass and occasionally when they passed an isolated farmhouse, children would come running out to wave at them. At last they turned on to another dirt road, which twisted and turned like a switchback up a heavily wooded hill. Here there was little sign of human presence apart from the road itself. Gum trees so tall that it made her dizzy to look at their canopies soared upwards from dense stands of bracken. The light was green, filtered, oddly mysterious. When she opened the window to let in some fresh air, it came rushing into the vehicle's interior, bringing with it the strong, damp aroma of the bush and the ceaseless whispering of the trees. Once a wallaby bounded across the road, disappearing in a flash of brown fur, and on another occasion Matt stopped to give way to an echidna,

which was busily shuffling across the road with its quills
lying flat like a neat pile of knitting needles on its back.
Otherwise they were completely alone until they emerged
on a ridge overlooking the sea and Matt turned into a
rutted driveway, which snaked up to the entrance of an
old weatherboard cottage. Its steeply pitched roof and
the tiny panes of glass in its windows showed that the
building was well over a hundred years old, but it had
been kept in good condition. The roof was new, the exterior weatherboards were painted white and there were
twin tubs of bright red geraniums on either side of the
steps leading up to the front veranda. Matt switched off
the ignition and gave Lisa a quizzical look.

'Let's put our gear inside and then go for a preliminary scout,' he suggested. 'I'll bring a rod and line
and see if I can catch something for lunch and you can
check out some likely sites for painting.'

'All right,' agreed Lisa.

Matt carried the heavy box of foodstuffs and Lisa followed him with the two small backpacks containing their
spare clothes. He had warned her that the cottage was
primitive, but she was unprepared for what she saw.
When he flung open the unlocked front door, she felt
as if she had stepped back in time. The walls were whitewashed, the floorboards were dark and warped with age
and a huge, handmade brick fireplace with a blackened
iron kettle and cooking griddle dominated one wall.
There was very little furniture and that, too, looked old.
A cedar gate-leg table and four carved chairs, an old-
fashioned couch and two deep armchairs recovered in a
tartan print. A hunting horn hung on the wall, not
looking like a self-conscious ornament, but rather a
useful instrument, which might be blown at any moment
to summon a family member from the forest or the beach

for a meal. Matt kicked off his elastic-sided boots at the
door and pushed them against the wall with his feet.

'We never wear shoes inside the cottage,' he explained
carelessly. 'They track in too much sand and leaf litter.
But you can do whatever you feel comfortable with.'

Lisa removed her shoes while Matt set down his box
of provisions on the dining table and crossed the room
to a rather lopsided door set in one wall. He turned the
brass handle and flung it open.

'This is the bedroom,' he announced. 'You can put
the packs in there, if you like.'

Reluctantly Lisa edged through the doorway behind
him. The room had an unpretentious charm, although
there was very little spare space in it. It was dominated
by a large, carved four-poster bed, covered with a
patchwork quilt in shades of crimson and dark green.
On either side of the bed were mahogany nightstands,
each one primly surmounted by a starched white cloth
with lace trim and an old-fashioned glass kerosene lamp.
Apart from the bed, there was no furniture in the room,
except for a plain blanket chest and an alcove curtained
in floral chintz, which evidently served as a makeshift
wardrobe. Even so, Lisa would have found the room
enchanting if it hadn't been for a nagging worry at the
back of her mind. What had Matt just said? 'This is the
bedroom'? Not 'one of the bedrooms' but 'the
bedroom'?

'Where are you planning to sleep?' she blurted
anxiously.

There was a glint of amusement in his eyes.

'I usually sleep in here, but I can make do with the
fold-out bed in the couch if that's what you'd prefer.'

'Yes. I would. Thank you,' she said disjointedly.
Dropping the two packs unceremoniously on the floor,

she wiped her sweating palms on her jeans. Somehow the atmosphere in this romantic little bedroom seemed suddenly suffocating. 'Can we go and see the rest of the house?'

'There's not much more to see,' said Matt, leading the way out of the room and into the living area. 'Only this lean-to section at the back.'

He ushered her into an enclosed porch, which ran the full width of the house. It was no more than four feet wide but to Lisa's relief she saw that it contained a perfectly adequate bathroom and a tiny but charming kitchen with a gas cook top and refrigerator and fitted benches of honey-coloured Huon pine. Yet something seemed to be missing. She looked around her slowly and suddenly realized what it was.

'No electricity?' she asked.

'No electricity,' he confirmed.

'What do you do at night-time?'

'Light the kerosene lamps. I rather like the soft glow, and for entertainment, well, I just listen to the howling of the wind and the roar of the sea and watch the pictures in the fire. Of course, if you're a TV addict, you may get painful withdrawal symptoms staying here for a week.'

She smiled at him. 'I'm not.'

'Good. So what do you think of the place?'

'It's beautiful,' she said sincerely. 'But so tiny!'

He gave a soft growl of laughter deep in the back of his throat.

'Would you believe me if I told you that the man who built it a hundred and thirty years ago married and raised a family of eight children here?'

Lisa's eyes widened.

'Really? They must have been packed in like sardines.'

He took a step closer, making her feel crowded in that tiny space. Although he didn't touch her, she could feel his eyes lingering on her as caressingly as if his warm fingers were tracing the contours of her face and neck.

'I think they believed in togetherness in those days,' he murmured. 'It's rather an inspiration, in a way, isn't it? Think of all the loving and sharing and quarrelling that went on under this roof. They had so little, those pioneering families, but perhaps they had everything that really matters.'

At any other time, Lisa might have agreed with him, but at the moment she felt too breathless and trapped to think straight. Her senses were reeling from his closeness, from the warmth of his body, from the faint, masculine odour of him that reminded her of spice and soap and leather. She took another step backwards and felt the hard edge of the wooden counter bump into her spine.

'Can't we go for our walk now?' she demanded.

She would have enjoyed that walk, if it hadn't been for Matt's disturbing presence. The cottage was set high on the ridge with a magnificent view over the bay. With her sketchbook and pencils in a canvas bag over her shoulder and a folding stool tucked under her arm, Lisa followed Matt down the rugged hillside and out to the empty foreshore. It was spectacularly beautiful and totally deserted. Waves crashed on the clean white sand, low sandstone cliffs sculpted by the action of the sea rose higher and higher until they gave way to thickets of dense, green trees. As they stepped over the last of the tangled grass leading to the foreshore, Matt suddenly jerked warningly on Lisa's sleeve.

'Careful,' he said.

Her heart lurched as she saw a fat, metallic-looking snake uncoil and glide away off the track just where she had been about to put her foot.

'What was it?' she asked unsteadily.

'A copperhead. They're very poisonous, although not as bad as tiger snakes. But don't worry, I'll look after you.'

I'll look after you. The words both touched and infuriated her. She must stop being so pathetic, looking on Matt as if he was some kind of old-fashioned pioneer who would protect and shelter her in this alarming wilderness. She didn't need his protection and she was perfectly capable of looking after herself! It was a comforting theory, but she found it hard to go on believing in it once Matt tried to teach her to fish. How was it that he ended up with several gleaming silvery fish within the first five minutes while Lisa couldn't even feel when the wretched things were biting? In the end she simply gave up in disgust, set up her folding stool and sketchpad and began to draw. After a while she forgot about trying to score off Matt and became absorbed in her work. It was very pleasant to sit there with the sun beating down on her, listening to the crash of the waves and the cries of the sea birds as she tried to capture the scene around her on paper.

Matt was equally absorbed. From time to time she glanced up and saw him casting his rod into the sea with an intense, expectant look on his face. He seemed so involved in what he was doing that he had probably forgotten all about her, but once his gaze met hers and he smiled briefly before turning back to the foaming waves. A wordless harmony seemed to stretch between them like an invisible bond linking them together. At last, satisfied with his catch, Matt came across the powdery white sand towards her.

'Would you like to have lunch here on the beach?' he asked. 'I could start a fire and we could fry the fish, if you like.'

Lisa stretched, squinted and put up one hand to massage her aching neck.

'Yes, please,' she agreed with pleasure. 'That would be wonderful. I hadn't realized it before, but I'm actually quite hungry. What time is it?'

Matt wasn't wearing a watch, but he looked up at the sun.

'About two o'clock,' he said.

Her eyes widened in amazement. 'Two o'clock! The time must have flown.'

It flew just as fast while Matt went about the preparations for their meal. Skilfully he built a small fire out of thin twigs and pieces of bark and lit it with a match from his backpack. Once the orange flames were licking and crackling into the air, he picked up the fish to clean them. Lisa wrinkled her nose and looked away while this messy task was being done. But once the fire was well alight and the fish were spluttering in a blackened old frying pan, her distaste vanished. In fact, the aroma was so delicious that she could hardly wait to eat.

'Don't sit there looking useless,' Matt chided her. 'There are plates and cutlery and a plastic container of salad in the bottom of my backpack. Make yourself useful and set the table, wench. Or should I say, set the groundsheet?'

She stuck out her tongue at his bossy tone, but a curious, bubbling feeling of happiness fizzed up inside her as she followed his instructions. I haven't had this much fun in years, she thought. The fried fish was de-

licious in its simple sauce of browned butter, parsley and
lemon and the salad of lettuce and tomato with French
dressing was equally good. When Matt produced a bottle
of Rhine Riesling and two long-stemmed wineglasses,
Lisa let out a contented noise like the purring of a cat.

'This is sheer bliss,' she said. 'I don't think I ever want
to go back to civilization.'

His eyes glinted. 'Be careful,' he warned. 'I might hold
you to that.'

She felt a mingled thrill of alarm and excitement at
his words, at their hint that he could somehow hold her
captive here and prevent her from going back to the real
world of noise and traffic and the constant struggle to
earn a living, the loneliness that sometimes crowded in
on her. A shadow crossed her face and her gaze was
wistful and distant as she accepted a glass of wine from
Matt.

'It's a nice thought,' she said in a brittle voice. 'But
sooner or later people have to face up to reality, don't
they?'

'Do they?' he countered. 'You make us sound like
passive victims who are just carried along by the tide of
events. I don't see it that way. I think we make our own
reality, our own choices about what we want our lives
to be. If you want to spend the rest of your life painting
on a beach like this, I see absolutely nothing to stop
you.'

She couldn't help feeling the irresistible force of his
personality as he spoke. It was as if he radiated an energy
a thousand times greater than other people's, as if he
could make anything happen by the sheer force of his
will. The thought alarmed and exhilarated her.

'You're an extraordinary person,' she said.

He clinked his glass against hers and then raised it in an ironic salute, his blue eyes scrutinizing her.

'No more extraordinary than you,' he replied, half to himself. 'I wonder what you really are, Lisa Hayward, and what you really want? I have a feeling that there's some mystery about you. Some secret that I'm going to have to discover.'

CHAPTER SIX

LISA dropped her gaze and took a hasty gulp of the white wine. It was as icy as a mountain stream, but it seemed to send a flood of fire coursing through her veins.

'There's no mystery about me,' she said hastily. 'No secrets. I'm perfectly ordinary.'

'Oh, hardly that,' replied Matt. 'I'd say you were utterly extraordinary.'

Her vanity made her fall straight into his trap.

'In what way?' she asked.

He smiled in the same quiet, triumphant way as when he had hooked those gleaming fish and brought them fighting and struggling into his grasp.

'You're extraordinarily infuriating. And extraordinarily attractive. And, unless I'm much mistaken, extraordinarily sensual.'

Lisa forgot all about the fact that she had intended to string Matt along and make him fall in love with her. This should have been a perfect chance for some highly charged flirtation, but instead of coming back with a provocative remark, she simply stared at him with a tormented expression.

'Don't say that,' she begged.

'Why not? It's the truth. You can't be unaware of how much you fascinate and infuriate me, Lisa. Something very powerful is going on between us and I'm sure you know it just as well as I do.'

She turned away from him, staring out at the turbulent sea.

'That's not true! There's nothing special between us, nothing special at all. You're just Tim's uncle and I'm——' her voice cracked, but she went on anyway '—and I'm nothing but an unimportant and very temporary guest.'

'Unimportant? Temporary?' he demanded in a harsh voice. 'I thought you were supposed to be marrying my nephew.'

'Then how can there be anything between us?' she cried, struggling to her feet with a jerky movement that upset her glass of wine. 'Look, Matt, leave me alone! Oh, I'll have to go back to Melbourne. I can't bear any more of this.'

'Just as you like,' he agreed indifferently.

Then he drained his own glass, packed the bag and fastidiously shook out the groundsheet. The spilt wine ran down it in runnels, its smell powerfully intoxicating. How like me to do that! thought Lisa bitterly. How like me to be awkward and emotional and careless of the consequences. I can't even drink a glass of wine without knocking it over!

'What are you thinking?' demanded Matt, gazing at her through narrowed eyes.

'Nothing important. Just that I'll always be the sort of person who blunders along, causing disaster, and you'll always be the sort of person who stands there with a little, disdainful smile, tidying up and staying aloof from it all. It must be nice never to make a mistake, never to get involved, never to do the wrong thing.'

Matt gave a harsh laugh.

'How little you know me,' he said.

Then with a swift angry movement he began cramming the stained groundsheet into the bag. Without a word he picked up his fishing rod and the rest of the fish and began striding up the track that led to the cottage. Lisa had to scurry to gather up her belongings and run after him, which annoyed her. She wasn't even sure why he was so hostile to her, but somehow this hurtful, angry silence was easier to bear than the dangerous attraction that kept flaring up between them. When they reached the cottage, they separated by common accord and Lisa set up her easel and sat down to soothe her jangled nerves by painting. Matt vanished into the back yard and chopped wood. When she went to make herself coffee, she looked out the kitchen window and saw him stripped to the waist, swinging the axe so that it bit deep into a massive log. After an hour his tanned, rippling back muscles were glistening with sweat and there was a large pile of neatly stacked firewood at the edge of the yard. Only when the sun set did he come inside to shower and change his clothes. Lisa was half dreading the long evening in each other's company without any distraction or hope of rescue, but she need not have worried. Matt's antagonism seemed to be firmly under control and, although he gazed at her once or twice with a strange, grim expression, he was perfectly pleasant to her. Once the fire was crackling in the hearth and the kerosene lamps were lit, they spent the rest of the evening playing Scrabble, as politely as if they were total strangers.

It was that remote, rather exaggerated courtesy that made it possible for Lisa to endure the rest of the week. Whatever hidden currents were running between them, Matt seemed just as determined as she was not to explore those murky depths. Occasionally the idea of trying to have her revenge flashed into Lisa's mind again, but she dismissed it. After all, she might be reckless, but she wasn't outright suicidal! Maybe one of these days she would have the courage to lead Matt on and pay him back for humiliating her, but not yet. Not until she was safely at the farm in the company of other people. But each day as they went out on their excursions, painting, fishing, bushwalking, and each night as they sat in the firelight talking and playing games, a feeling of restless tension began to build and build inside her, like the hushed expectancy when a tropical storm is brewing. On the last night before they were due to leave, matters came to a head. They were sitting at the table with port and coffee at their elbows playing a game of Monopoly in the soft golden glow from the kerosene lamp. Matt, as always, played with a mixture of shrewdness and daring that exasperated Lisa. At last, when he had stripped her of almost everything she possessed, she flung up her hands with an exaggerated groan and dropped the dice.

'All right, that's it,' she said humorously. 'I'll admit defeat. I don't care about money, anyway.'

Matt sipped his port, swirled it on his tongue and then swallowed.

'And yet you're going to marry Tim to get it,' he said unpleasantly.

Suddenly the atmosphere, which had been friendly and bantering earlier in the evening, had a nasty, dangerous edge to it.

'What of it?' retorted Lisa.

'What of it? Well, you admit you don't love him and you're only doing it out of greed. That's fairly despicable, isn't it? Doesn't it ever give you a twinge of conscience?'

Lisa's eyes flashed angrily. How dare he lecture her about what was despicable and what wasn't? What about his own behaviour with Andrea?

'Oh, so you're the soul of honour yourself, are you?' she jeered. 'I don't see that it's any business of yours what I do with Tim! But no, as a matter of fact I don't feel any twinge of conscience about it.'

She tossed down a gulp of port and choked on its fiery sweetness. For a moment it scarcely seemed to matter that she had no genuine intention of marrying Tim anyway. What did matter was that she was under attack from Matt Lansdon, and for some ridiculous reason his contempt cut her to the bone.

'As far as I can see, Tim is getting a perfectly reasonable bargain,' she continued in a rapid, angry voice. 'I'm very fond of him, we get along well together, I don't intend to hurt him in any way. So why shouldn't I marry him?'

'But you don't love him, do you?' insisted Matt. 'I'm willing to bet you don't even find him very physically exciting, do you? Do you?'

Lisa's head jerked up as if he had slapped her face. For a moment the image of Tim swam before her eyes and she felt the mixture of affection and irritation that her feckless young flatmate had always aroused in her. Of course she didn't find him physically exciting! The mere thought was ridiculous. But she did care about him. These unspoken thoughts showed in her face, and she detected a glint of scornful triumph in Matt's eyes.

'Well, even if I don't find him physically exciting, what of it?' she challenged. 'Does it matter?'

'Of course it matters,' he snarled. 'There are moments in anybody's life when it seems to be the only thing that does matter.' He didn't touch her, but his glance was so heated that she shrank back as if she had been scorched. 'If that sort of violent attraction doesn't exist within a marriage, you can be damn sure that sooner or later it will happen outside it. At times like that, unless people have a really solid relationship founded on love, they can easily lose their heads. They do crazy, destructive things that hurt their innocent partners. You admit that you don't love Tim, that you're not even sexually attracted to him. So what will you do if you meet some other man who does attract you?'

Every muscle in his body seemed to be tensed and she could see the pulse in his throat, throbbing violently as he leaned across the table towards her with his mouth set in a grim line. Suddenly she knew without a shadow of doubt what this conversation was about. A breathless, almost suffocating sense of panic overwhelmed her as she tried to fight the relentless tug of her attraction to him.

'It could be a problem,' she admitted hoarsely. 'I don't know what I'd do.'

Shakily she rose to her feet, intending to move away, to put distance between them, but Matt thwarted her by rising also and blocking her way. She looked at him, but that was a mistake. The naked, hungry desire in his eyes only made her heart beat more wildly than ever. Mesmerised, she leaned towards him, aching, yearning, wanting him. Her fingers closed convulsively on his sleeve. For one defiant moment she tried to tell herself that she was only doing this to lead him on, to have her revenge for his outrageous behaviour. But when he suddenly cupped her face in his hands and pressed a long brutal devouring kiss on her lips, she knew she was wrong. Her whole body was on fire, throbbing with hunger for him. Who was she kidding? She wasn't kissing him because she wanted to punish him, she was doing it because she craved him, needed him, loved him, however badly he had treated her.

She arched her back so that her breasts rubbed against his chest. When his right hand sought and stroked her nipple, she let out a faint moan and pressed herself closer against him, shuddering with pleasure under his touch. And all the while his skilful maddening hands moved over her shoulders and breasts and spine in a rhythm of caresses that was driving her frantic. Slowly, appreciatively he unbuttoned her shirt, revealing the lavish contours of her body. Hypnotised, she moved like a dancer in his arms and buried her head in his shoulder as he slipped the garment off and threw it on the ground. She felt his lips brush against the bare skin of her neck and caught her breath. While she was still standing rigid and tense with yearning, his fingers skilfully unfastened her bra. That, too, was tossed to the floor, and then his hands cupped her warm, heaving breasts.

'You are so beautiful, Lisa,' he murmured into the scented cloud of her hair. 'I've wanted you from the first moment I saw you.'

With a swift movement he swept her into his arms and carried her through to the bedroom. She opened her mouth to protest and found it stopped by another of those long, devouring kisses that sent tingles of excitement sparking through her body. Through half-closed eyelids she saw their shadows loom up on the far wall in the lamplight, then Matt thrust her into the downy softness of the pillows. There was no longer any pretence of indifference in either of them. As his lean, hard, masculine strength crushed her into the bed and she felt the heat of his body against her skin, she uttered another soft moan of arousal and her eyes closed completely. Her lips felt warm and moist and swollen as she surrendered utterly to his kisses. Winding her legs around him and thrusting her fingers into his thick, silky hair, she drew him tighter against her, glorying in the tough, warm, virile pressure of his weight upon her.

'Oh, Matt,' she breathed with a convulsive shudder as his fingers crept down and began stroking her intimately. 'Oh, Matt...yes. Yes!'

He reared up for a moment, kneeling astride her, with his breath coming in fast, erratic gulps as he unbuttoned his shirt and hauled it over his head. Her eyes flew open and she gazed at him in wonder, unable to imagine anything more magnificent than that superb, masculine body. Honed by years of hard, physical labour, the muscles in his massive shoulders and chest bunched like steel cables under the skin as he moved. Then he flung the shirt aside and looked down at her. His expression was so intense, so searing, so shamelessly possessive that Lisa felt her whole body quiver. Something deep inside her seemed to melt and flutter and throb under that relentless masculine scrutiny. She was conscious of a primitive, urgent longing to be seized and entered fiercely, taken again and again until she was totally his. All her independence, her schemes for revenge, her resistance were like a shield made of tissue paper. It crumpled uselessly, leaving her utterly defenceless.

Seeing the harsh glint of triumph and resolve in his stormy features, she felt her whole body throb with a moist, burning need for him. And he sensed it. She knew that. She saw it in his savage, gloating smile, in the way he suddenly pinioned her wrists and flung himself down on her, deliberately grinding his pelvis against hers so that she had no doubt at all what he wanted. Their kisses were no longer gentle, but stormy, passionate, turbulent. They rolled wildly together, clutching at each other with frenzied fingers and gasping for air in brief, reluctant truces. She had never known that such intense, physical passion could be possible, never guessed that she could feel such an inferno of unsatisfied longing.

Their clothes seemed like a senseless barrier to the total union that she craved more urgently with each escalating heartbeat. Yet when his hands went roughly to the waistband of her jeans and he tore open the zip, she was shocked at last into resistance.

'No!' she gasped, sitting up and shuddering.

He ignored her. His body was gleaming with sweat, his muscles were tensed and a pulse was hammering frantically in his throat. With a sudden, savage intensity he wrenched off her jeans and caught his breath. His eyes glazed with an angry, yearning look of anticipation and she saw his tongue moisten his lower lip.

'No!' she cried again, her voice sharp with alarm.

He shook his head, as if she was talking a foreign language.

'But you want this,' he murmured hoarsely. 'Damn you, Lisa, you want this as badly as I do!'

'N-no,' she stuttered, shrinking from him, retreating against the wall. 'No, I don't.'

His only response was to thrust his hand into the most intimate part of her. She gave a small, muffled cry that was half protest and half pleasure, then he raised his glistening fingers contemptuously at her.

'You may lie, but your body doesn't!' he said. 'I don't know what the hell this is about, but if you've got a shred of honesty, at least admit this. You want me, Lisa!'

She flinched at the anger in his voice and, drawing up her knees, scrambled awkwardly under the covers. Then she let out a long, shuddering sigh, tried twice to speak and failed.

'Lisa,' he growled, gripping her by the shoulders and holding her so close that their foreheads were touching, their breath mingled. 'You're not frightened of me, are you?'

She shook her head, biting her lower lip to keep back the baffling threat of tears. Not of him, no. Of herself, maybe. Her feelings. The enormity of what they had been on the verge of doing. Her throat was so tight, she could hardly force the words out.

'No,' she muttered at last.

'Then tell me the truth. Do you want me or not?'

The truth, she thought bitterly. The truth was so complicated she doubted if they would ever unravel it. Andrea. Tim. Her own wildly unstable feelings about Matt. Her yearning for love, commitment, not just sex.

'Yes, I want you,' she flared. 'Of course I want you. But I can't go through with it, Matt. I can't bear to make love with you.'

He held her tightly. So tightly that he must have been aware of the way her whole body was shaking as if she had a fever, must have been aware of that dreadful, brief, whimpering sound that she made deep in the back of her throat when he kissed the top of her head.

'Why not?' he demanded.

She took a long, shuddering breath and pushed him resolutely away.

'Because I'll lose any self-respect I ever had if we make love now, Matt.'

The silence seemed to lengthen agonizingly between them. Lisa crouched motionless as if she were carved out of stone, unable to drag her eyes away from Matt's face. Yet she could not interpret what she saw there. Outrage? Shock? Anger? Perhaps even a wry glimmer of approval? At last he gave a harsh sigh and a sudden tremor went through his limbs as if he was a weight-lifter setting down an intolerably heavy burden. Stony-faced and expressionless, he climbed off the bed and stood gazing down at her.

'Get dressed and pack your things,' he said curtly. 'We're going home.'

'Now?' she asked. 'But it's after midnight. The road——'

'Yes, now,' he rapped out, clenching his fist so tightly around the bedpost that she thought he would snap it right through. 'Be ready when I come back.'

He did not say where he was going, but released his grip on the bedpost and strode blindly out of the room, pausing only to pick up his shirt as he left. She heard a clatter in the other room as if he had dropped one of his boots, followed by a muffled swearing. Then the front door slammed so loudly that the bedroom walls reverberated. As if she was in a trance, Lisa got out of bed and began assembling her clothes. She felt shaken, disoriented, unable to take in what had happened between them. It was as if she had just emerged from a traffic accident, still retaining the trembling power of movement, but unable yet to speak or feel. And in some crazy way Matt's pronouncement that they would have to leave made sense to her. Perhaps when they were away from this dangerous place with its orange firelight and whispering trees and huge, star-studded sky and roaring ocean, they would come to their senses. This whole insane episode might weaken and evaporate like a bad dream.

'Oh, heavens, I hope so,' she whispered fervently as she stumbled into the living room, picked up her discarded shirt and buried her face in its scented folds. 'How can I face him again otherwise?'

Yet when Matt returned half an hour later, it was like meeting a stranger. There was no longer any tension or rage or urgency in his manner. Instead, he wore a cool, ironical smile and moved around the cottage as casually as if it was nine o'clock in the morning and he was simply putting things in order after a rather uneventful fishing trip. Feeling deeply embarrassed and self-conscious, Lisa at last shuffled into the living room and set the two backpacks on the floor. Without raising her eyes, she spoke.

'I've packed up all the——' To her chagrin, her voice squeaked, so that she had to clear her throat and try again. 'I've packed up all the food that was in the kitchen.'

'Good,' said Matt pleasantly. 'I hope you got the fresh fish I caught today. Tim's very fond of fish.'

Incredulously Lisa's eyes flew up to meet his, but he was already turning away from her. Was that all he intended to say to her? Were they going to have some conspiracy of silence, to pretend that the whole thing had never happened? Well, in theory that might be the best thing, but how could he do it? How could he simply close the door on an emotional drama like that and pretend it had never happened? And then the bitter thought came to her. Well, he managed it with Andrea, didn't he?

All the way to the farm, she sat in a hurt and apprehensive silence, while Matt guided the vehicle tranquilly down the dark, treacherous roads. Occasionally they saw the red, glowing eyes of possums in the trees overhead and once she heard the barking growl of a Tasmanian devil out on the hunting trail. The loneliness and strangeness of this unfamiliar world no longer seemed fascinating, but oppressive and frightening. It was just as hostile and unwelcoming as the man who sat so close and yet so far from her, his grim features eerily lit by moonlight, barred with the shadows of passing branches. It was a relief when at last they turned on to a metalled road and saw a friendly yellow light on the porch of a distant farmhouse. Softly, perhaps unconsciously, Matt began to whistle under his breath. An aria from *Carmen*. Lisa winced and closed her eyes.

The next morning at breakfast Matt made no reference to anything that had passed between them. He was the perfect host, hospitable, pleasant, but unmistakably formal.

'I'm going to move some stock from the top paddock today, Tim,' he announced. 'I thought you might be interested in helping me.'

Tim hunched his shoulders and a sulky expression flitted across his face. Lisa knew that if she didn't intervene, he would dream up some far-fetched story that would plunge her into another lot of trouble.

'Actually, Tim and I have other plans,' she cut in. 'I was planning to give him a painting lesson today, unless you have some objections, Matt?'

'Why should I have any objections?' asked Matt, meeting her eyes but looking through her as if she wasn't really there.

'Good. Well, if you've no objections, we thought we might use the old cottage over the hill as a studio. It is Tim's property, after all, but we thought we ought to ask you since you're used to being in charge around here.'

There was an unmistakable note of malice in Lisa's voice as she said this, but Matt didn't give her the satisfaction of rising to the bait. Apart from a faint frown, he gave no sign of having absorbed a word she had said.

'Do as you please,' he said indifferently and with a cool nod to both of them, he left the room.

'Why did you say that about the painting lessons?' grumbled Tim the moment his uncle had left the room.

'He's going to realize what I'm doing if you don't watch out.'

'Oh, stop complaining,' snapped Lisa. 'You've had your week to work on your painting uninterrupted and now you've got official permission to use the cottage as a studio into the bargain. What more do you want?'

'The Buller Prize,' replied Tim, pressing his hands together in prayer and raising his eyes soulfully.

'Then we'd better get to work. How's the painting coming along, anyway?'

'Not too badly, as a matter of fact. I've been working about eighteen hours a day on it while you were away, but I can't quite capture the quality of the light the way I want it. And the right shoulder looks distorted somehow. I wish you'd have a look at it for me.'

Lisa found a welcome break from her own problems in helping Tim with his work. His talent dazzled her. The moment she saw the canvas, she felt an almost reverent certainty that the finished painting was going to be a masterpiece. Tim had always shown promise, but this wasn't just promise, it was mature artistic achievement. And now that he had a genuine goal to work towards, he seemed ready to give up the juvenile time wasting, which had irritated her so much in the past. There were still technical points he needed to learn, but he was prepared to work like a demon to acquire them. And his absorption was so profound that he would quite happily go without meals or sleep or any kind of relaxation in order to get his masterpiece finished. In the past Lisa had had to bully him to keep going with his projects, but now she had to bully him to make him stop. Otherwise he would have burnt himself out with sheer nervous energy. Well, at least it had the advantage that Tim was far too consumed by his own concerns to ask her what had happened on her week away with Matt. And it was doubtful whether he even noticed the coolness between his uncle and his friend. It was left to Lisa to raise the subject in a roundabout fashion two days after her return from Fortescue Bay.

'Tim, do you think I ought to go back to Melbourne?' she blurted out.

He stared at her in consternation and a blob of green acrylic paint dripped off his brush and on to the knee of his jeans.

'Don't be stupid, I need you here. Who's going to help me with my brushwork if you leave? Besides, you promised you'd stay until after Christmas! Why on earth do you want to go?'

She flushed uncomfortably and dropped her eyes.

'Well, I don't think Matt likes me much,' she said. 'I feel awkward about staying.'

'What's that got to do with anything?' asked Tim. 'He doesn't like me much, either, but I'm still here, aren't I?' A sudden inspiration seized him. 'Anyway, I'm the legal owner of this property, not Matt! And I'm asking you to stay, so for heaven's sake shut up and let me get on with my work.'

Lisa grinned and gave in. The truth was that she didn't want to leave, in spite of the strange ache in her chest whenever she crossed Matt's path by accident. Common sense told her she would be wiser to make a complete break, but deep down she didn't want to be sensible. It was easier to use Tim's needs as her excuse for doing what she wanted to do, anyway. It might be madness, but at least she could have these last few days in Matt's company before she said goodbye to him forever.

Tim had been half afraid at the beginning that Matt would burst in on them at the cottage, but as two weeks passed and then a third, he began to relax. Lisa tried several times to persuade him to tell his uncle the truth, but he always stubbornly refused.

'I'll tell him once the painting is finished and submitted to the judging committee,' he replied. 'I don't want any flak from him or my mother until that's safely over.'

'But you've failed all your university exams, Tim,' said Lisa. 'You can't hide that from them forever. Isn't it better to come clean, tell Matt you hate economics and you want to study art? Give him the chance to discuss the matter with you? You never know, he might be reasonable about it.'

'Like hell he will! No, Lisa, I'm not going to be pushed around by you on this. Anyway, it won't be long now until Christmas is over, the painting is finished and we can both go back to Melbourne. And if I get the scholarship, I can just jet off to Paris, can't I?'

'Without explaining anything to Matt?' demanded Lisa in an outraged voice. 'I think that's really unspeakable! He's done his best to be a good trustee for you.'

'Whose side are you on? I thought you didn't even like him! Hell, Lisa, look what you've made me do! I've got the line of that shoulder completely wrong again.'

Several minutes of grumbling and fussing around with turpentine and rags didn't make things any better. Tim sucked on the end of his paintbrush and squinted at her thoughtfully.

'Couldn't you just strip off and hop up on the bed for me? I need to see the angle to get it right.'

Lisa squirmed.

'I don't want to do that any more,' she said.

He stared at her in astonishment.

'Why on earth not? You always did before. Lisa, you're not worried that I'm going to grope you or something, are you? Because, look, no offence, but I find you incredibly unattractive.'

'Thanks,' said Lisa dryly. 'No offence. Sure. No, Tim, I am not afraid that you're going to grope me, I just don't want to do it. It's...it's too cold in here to take my clothes off.'

'Well, just your top,' pleaded Tim. 'You can leave your underwear on. That won't really affect the shoulder line too much. Oh, come on, Lisa.'

With a feeling of vague misgiving, Lisa took off her top and allowed Tim to arrange her precisely in the middle of the large double bed. She wished he hadn't chosen the bedroom as his studio, but they had both agreed that it was the only room where the light was right.

'Keep still,' he warned.

They were so preoccupied that they paid no attention to the sound of a vehicle coming along the rough farm track. Probably just Ron Barwick on his way out to check the sheep. Then there was the sound of a peremptory knocking at the back door, and footsteps echoed in the kitchen.

'Tim, are you there?'

'Hell!' groaned Tim. 'It's Matt! Don't let him see what I'm doing, Lisa. I'll go out and try to stall him.'

Lisa scrambled up as Tim vanished out the bedroom door. Lifting the easel gingerly, she lugged the wet painting behind the Chinese screen in one corner of the room. In a few frantic seconds the brushes and paints followed suit. Then she had just enough time to pull her top on before the door burst open and Matt came striding into the room. He looked her up and down with a grim expression.

'I just came down to tell you both that Sonia has arrived,' he announced, spitting out the words like bullets. 'I dare say you will want to get tidied up and come and greet your future mother-in-law, Lisa. You and Tim can come along with me now in the four-wheel drive. Oh, by the way, did you know that you're wearing your top inside out?'

In spite of the thirty-degree heat, the atmosphere was distinctly chilly in the four-wheel drive vehicle as they headed to the main farmhouse, and it didn't grow any warmer when they entered the living room and found Tim's mother sitting on the sofa sipping soda water and tapping her fingers restlessly. Her mouth tightened at the sight of Lisa and she didn't seem much happier to be reunited with her son. A faint, exasperated sigh escaped her as her gaze tracked down over Tim's long, uncombed hair and paint-spattered clothes. With the air of someone reluctantly conscripted from the crowd to kiss a sea lion at a marine park performance, she endured Tim's embrace. Then she held him at arm's length and examined him disparagingly. Her obvious disapproval made Lisa smother a grin, for there was actually a considerable resemblance between mother and son.

Sonia had the same butter-coloured hair as Tim, which framed her face in a silken bell. Their chiselled features and regular teeth were also remarkably similar, but the main difference was in their eyes. Where Tim's were brown and alight with warmth, Sonia's were grey and cold beneath the heavy mascara that clogged her lashes. Mutton dressed as lamb, thought Lisa sourly, glancing at Sonia's youthfully styled, sleeveless white dress, which showed off her dazzling tan. All the same, she had to admit that Sonia was still extremely pretty, in spite of her petulant mouth and the fine web of tiny lines beginning to appear at the corners of her eyes. Her waist was only about half the size of Lisa's and was cinched in tightly with a scarlet leather belt that matched her fingernails, shoes and the beads around her throat. Yet somehow the air of glossy perfection was marred by the spite that radiated from the older woman's face as she returned Lisa's gaze.

'What a surprise to see you!' she exclaimed, giving Lisa a look that made her feel like a bag of fish heads that had been left in the sun too long. 'What are you doing here?'

Tim's mouth hardened at his mother's tone and he flung his arm deliberately around Lisa's shoulders.

'I invited her,' he retorted. 'After all, she's practically one of the family.'

Sonia gave an unconvincing trill of laughter.

'Really? But, Tim, darling, you mustn't forget that this is Matt's home, even though the place does belong to you. It's hardly polite for you to invite guests without consulting him.'

To Lisa's surprise Matt intervened in her defence. She had no illusions about the fact that he was coldly furious with her, but there was a warning flash in his blue eyes as he turned to Sonia.

'Lisa is my guest, too,' he said in a hard voice. 'And it's hardly polite for us to talk about her as if she's not present. Now, Lisa and Tim, do sit down and have a drink while Sonia tells us about her plans.'

Over more soda water, chilled orange juice and nuts, Sonia outlined her programme for the rest of the day.

'I must drive Tim up to town for a haircut and some new clothes. You're an absolute disgrace, darling. It's

Christmas Day tomorrow and I want you to look nice with all the family coming for Christmas dinner. You know Patricia likes you to dress up, and Alison's young people always look so smart. Even Helen does her best with her little boys, poor thing.'

Lisa felt a spurt of annoyance as Sonia went on talking about people she had never met, deliberately excluding her from the conversation. But once again Matt came to the rescue.

'These are all family members who are coming for Christmas dinner tomorrow,' he explained with a slight twist of his lips, which might have been a smile. 'Patricia is my mother, Alison is my sister and Helen is my cousin Graham's widow.'

'Was Graham the one you told me about who was lost at sea from the tuna fleet?' asked Lisa, seizing gratefully on a detail she recognized.

'Yes.'

Sonia was momentarily disconcerted by this collusion between Matt and Lisa, but she soon continued gamely.

'We'll have quite a crowd, Matt. Goodness, eleven all together. You, me, Tim, Patricia, Helen and her two boys and Alison, Brendan and their two.'

'Twelve,' said Matt stonily. 'You're forgetting Lisa.'

'Oh, how silly of me! Well, I do hope your housekeeper is up to the job. But I suppose Lisa will help her out, won't you, my dear? I'm sure that after enjoying such a long holiday here you'll want to make yourself useful.'

Lisa almost ground her teeth at Sonia's patronizing tone, but kept her temper with difficulty.

'Of course,' she agreed sweetly. 'But I'll be surprised if Judy needs any help. She's always so well organized.'

Yet that was just where she was wrong. Ten minutes later, while Sonia was cross-examining an evasive Tim about the strange lateness of his exam results, the telephone rang and shortly afterwards an excited Judy Barwick burst into the room.

'Oh, Matt, you could have knocked me down with a feather! Do you know who that was on the telephone? My son Darrell! Can you imagine? He's been travelling around Europe for the last three years and now he's decided to come home for Christmas and surprise us.'

'That's wonderful news, Judy,' said Matt warmly. 'When's he arriving?'

'He's in Melbourne right now, but all the flights to Tasmania are booked out until tomorrow morning. What I was wondering was whether I could drive to the airport to meet him first thing. It would mean I'd have to start work a bit late, but I'm sure I could still have your Christmas dinner ready in time.'

'Oh, Judy, I don't like to think of you coming here to cook for us when you should be home with your son,' protested Matt. 'Perhaps——'

'I'll cook the Christmas dinner,' offered Lisa impulsively. She liked Judy. Besides, it would be a way of blotting out some of the unwelcome debt she owed Matt after being his guest for so long. What was more, it would take her out of Sonia's firing line. Not that she feared Tim's mother, but it seemed unfair to let their mutual hostility spoil Christmas for the rest of the family. 'You just tell me what to do.'

They vanished into the kitchen together.

'That was good of you, Lisa,' said Matt when Lisa finally returned alone.

'Absolutely sweet of you,' agreed Sonia. 'Of course, you've had a lot of experience at that sort of thing, haven't you? Tim told me how you used to work as a waitress in that delightfully squalid little pizza parlour down in Lygon Street. Well, Tim, you and I must fly if we're going to do our shopping in town. I'd invite you to come, Lisa, but I suppose you're going to be too busy for the rest of the day, scrubbing floors and baking mince pies. What about you, Matt? Will you come with us?'

'No, thank you,' said Matt curtly.

When mother and son had finally vanished in Matt's red Porsche surrounded by a cloud of dust, Lisa found herself in a situation she had dreaded. Alone with Matt. Hostility still radiated out from him in a toxic cloud, so she was surprised by his first words.

'Don't let Sonia upset you,' he growled. 'She's an insensitive, shallow woman who is entirely too fond of the sound of her own voice, but I can assure you that the rest of my family will treat you with far more consideration.'

Lisa shrugged.

'Thanks, but it doesn't really matter. In any case, it's all so farcical. If only Sonia knew, she has nothing to——' She broke off, suddenly realizing that she was on the verge of betraying herself. 'Well, I must go and start cooking.'

Matt's brows met in a thoughtful scowl, but he didn't attempt to follow her and she was half disappointed, half grateful. The rest of the day flew by as she thawed the turkey, made the stuffing, set the dining room table and baked two large batches of mince pies. She heard Matt leave the house and return some time later. He seemed to be pacing round in the living room, and there was the sound of hammering. Shortly after six o'clock, consumed by an unwilling curiosity, she went in with a plate of mince pies.

'Would you like to try my——? Oh! Is that where you've been? Cutting down a Christmas tree?'

The room was full of the aromatic scent of pine resin and she felt a few springy needles underfoot as she walked across the carpet. Matt had just finished nailing an X-shaped base to the trunk of a huge tree and now he hauled it upright and set it in a corner. Then he accepted one of her mince pies, warm, crusty and oozing with sticky fruit. Lisa watched proudly as his eyebrows went up and he nodded.

'Not bad,' he said grudgingly. 'I suppose I ought to offer you a sherry.'

He walked to the sideboard and came back with two glasses of Flor Fino sherry.

'Happy Christmas,' he muttered.

'Happy Christmas,' echoed Lisa, touching the rim of her crystal glass against his. She felt an obscure pain under her heart as their eyes met. He hates me, she thought despairingly. And I distrust him. And yet... Matt's blue eyes were fixed stormily on hers. Suddenly with an abrupt movement he turned away from her and strode across the room. At first she thought that he was abandoning her, and disappointment pierced through her like the thrust of a knife. Then he set down his empty glass and rammed a cassette brutally into the recorder. There was a brief pause before the sweet, poignant sound of a boys' choir singing Christmas carols swept into the room.

'You could stay and decorate the tree with me, if you like,' he muttered over his shoulder.

They worked together in silence, hanging fairy lights, red and green and blue, from the branches. After that they added striped candy canes and strings of tinsel and coloured balls. Lisa had no illusions about the hostility that still vibrated between them, but she was aware of something else. Perhaps the bittersweet longing for harmony that had prompted enemy soldiers in World War One to lay down their arms at Christmas and call a truce. When Matt climbed the stepladder and demanded the gold star for the top of the tree, she held it up to him with all her longing shimmering in her eyes. He fastened it to the topmost branch without even looking at her, then his gaze fixed angrily on her. Suddenly he caught a great fistful of her rippling auburn hair.

'Lisa,' he growled.

There was a sound in the doorway. Lisa turned her head and gave a cry as Matt's grip pulled her up short. Standing there in the winking glow of the Christmas lights were a woman and a child. The woman stepped forward, and Lisa felt an ominous sense of impending disaster.

'Andrea!' said Matt sharply. 'What are you doing here?'

Even in the half light from the Christmas tree, Lisa could see that the woman was deeply distressed. She put out her hands in a pleading gesture.

'I forgot... to thaw out our turkey, Matt,' she said in a rush. 'And I so badly wanted Justin to have a proper Christmas. Couldn't we come to your place tomorrow? Just this once? Please, please, please!'

A lump rose in Lisa's throat and her eyes prickled, but to her incredulous horror Matt was grabbing Andrea by the arm and bundling her out the way she had come. Pausing only to snatch a few candy canes and thrust them into Justin's hands, he pushed them both ruthlessly out through the French doors. His voice was low, but not too low for Lisa to catch his words.

'No, Andrea, I've told you before. I'm sorry about your problems, but I won't allow you to come here and ruin Christmas for the rest of my family! You chose to act as you did and you'll have to bear the consequences.'

CHAPTER SEVEN

FOR a moment Lisa stood frozen to the spot, unable to move with the shock and anger she felt. Then suddenly the power of movement came surging into her trembling legs and she raced outside just in time to see Andrea dragging Justin by the hand towards her car, wiping her eyes as she went. Lisa ran after her.

'Wait,' she called, but Andrea shook her off.

Still racked by sobs, the young mother thrust her son into the car like a parcel, did up his seat belt and slammed the door. Then she ran around to the driver's side, climbed in and drove away.

'How could you do that to her?' burst out Lisa as she watched the car vanish down the dusty driveway.

Matt's face was as hard as if it were carved out of solid granite. A brooding expression narrowed his eyes and lent a bitter twist to his mouth.

'You know nothing about it!' he said savagely. 'Who are you to set yourself up as judge and jury about what I've done?'

Lisa stared at him, aghast, unable to believe in his brutality. Unable to believe that he could be so insensitive to the way she felt about him.

'Oh, I'm nobody!' she flared, completely forgetting her role as Tim's fiancée in her outrage. 'Nobody at all, I know that. I'm just a total outsider who'll be leaving here forever in a couple of days! So I don't have any right to care about what you do, to get upset when you—to...oh, what's the use?'

With a choking sob she ran inside the house and slammed the door, then bolted for the stairs and the sanctuary of her bedroom. Once there she locked herself in and slumped on the bed. Cold shudders kept overtaking her as if she had malaria.

'How could he?' she breathed incredulously, hugging her arms around her body and rocking back and forth. 'How could he be so cruel? Is that what he'd do to me if I was fool enough to sleep with him?'

Except that she wouldn't be fool enough! She wouldn't give in to his dangerous, mesmerising charm. And yet it wasn't charm, exactly. Lisa had always thought of charm as something rather slippery and shallow and unreliable, whereas Matt's brand of magnetism was something as powerful and stable as a rock. Which was what made his betrayal of Andrea so inexplicable. It seemed completely out of character for Matt to have abandoned his own child and its mother when he had always seemed to value family loyalty and tradition so highly. And yet there it was—that discordant, baffling evidence that Matt was glib and untrustworthy. It hurt her horribly to realize that he was so callous and manipulative and insincere. Why had she ever let him stir her so profoundly?

She half hoped and half feared that he might follow her to her room and confront her with a quarrel, which would clear the air and produce some magical explanation for his actions. But he didn't. And after a long time, Lisa heard the sound of the Porsche bringing Sonia and Tim back from their shopping expedition. She didn't feel like facing Sonia again, so she stayed upstairs and was relieved when nobody came up to ask her if she wanted dinner. Then shortly before midnight there was a tap on her door. It was too light and excitable to be

Matt. Half asleep by this time, Lisa blinked and dragged herself off the bed.

'Tim,' she said listlessly, opening the door.

He burst inside, looking as radiant as a lighthouse. His hair was neatly cut and he wore expensive new sports clothes.

'Guess what? It's finished!'

'What's finished?'

'The painting, of course. I've just spent the last two hours down there. I've changed into my good clothes so Mum wouldn't nag or get suspicious, but she and Matt have both gone off to bed. Do you want to come and see it?'

'Now?'

'Yes. Tomorrow there'll be Christmas dinner and relatives everywhere and not a chance to move. And as soon as the paint is dry after that, I'm off! I'm flying to Melbourne to take it to the judges. So you've got to come now, Lisa.'

Lisa had dozed off in her clothes, so there was no need to get dressed. She simply combed her fingers through her hair and followed Tim downstairs with a troubled frown. As they lurched down the rough track in the dark, hitting every bump with the four-wheel drive vehicle, the wry thought occurred to her that she was very glad she wasn't planning to marry Tim. He was phenomenally self-absorbed and totally different from his uncle. Not that Matt was easy to get along with, either! But she always felt that his occasional abrasive rudeness was due to powerful, deep-rooted feelings towards her. She never felt that he was simply oblivious to her existence. He was never just blithely selfish like Tim.

'Well, what do you think?' asked Tim a few minutes later.

Lisa was silent for a moment, scarcely able to believe what she was seeing.

'It's magnificent,' she admitted. 'It reminds me of Lucien Freud's work. The brush strokes are really fresh and vigorous and you haven't overworked your mixing before you put the paint on the canvas, so the colours don't look muddy. And the quality of the light is wonderful.'

'Good. Then maybe it will win the Buller Prize and I can shoot off overseas without ever having to explain to Matt and my mother why I failed all my exams.'

'Tim, that's totally irresponsible. You can't just go off without a word of explanation to Matt. Whatever else he may be, he's been a good trustee to you. You owe him some kind of family loyalty.'

'Cut it out, Lisa. You sound just like him. Responsibility! Loyalty! You'd make a good pair.'

'No, we wouldn't!'

'Anyway, I'm not telling him and don't you dare say a word, either, or I'll murder you.'

Lisa had little time to worry about Tim's secrets the following day. She was too busy racing around in the kitchen. She did feel a few nervous flutters about the prospect of encountering Matt again, but he seemed to be deliberately staying out of her way. By the time the other family members began arriving at noon, the house was full of the delectable smell of roast turkey, baked potatoes, gravy and vegetables. Lisa was wearing a new dress of vivid, flame-coloured silk and had her hair tied back to show off her favourite gold earrings and necklace. All the same, for once in her life she was rather hoping to lurk in the background like Cinderella. But she should have known that Matt would insist on tormenting her. He arrived in the kitchen just as she was bending, red-faced and flustered, to baste the turkey. She almost dropped the basting spoon in her confusion at the sight of him. He was sprucely dressed in light-weight grey slacks and a short-sleeved, blue striped shirt, and his face wore the faintly mocking smile that she had disliked so much at their first encounter. He spoke as if the previous evening scene with Andrea had never happened.

'Do you need any help there?'

'No, thanks. I've nearly finished.'

'Good. Then come and meet the rest of the family.'

There seemed to be no escape, so Lisa snatched off her apron, tidied her hair and followed Matt with the expression of a martyr on her way to execution. When she found herself in the living room, she was pleasantly surprised by her reception. Of course, that was partly because Matt was busy being the perfect host in a way that made her long to kick him.

'Lisa, let me introduce you to my mother, Patricia, my sister, Alison, and her husband, Brendan Courtney, and their kids, Steven and Hilary. Now, what can I get you to drink? Gin and tonic? Tim, there's the doorbell again. You're the closest, will you go?'

There was a fresh round of introductions as a brown-haired woman in her mid-thirties arrived with two unruly boys of about nine and eleven. This must be Graham's widow, thought Lisa, trying to place her in the family. I wonder if she always looks so gloomy? Never shy by nature, Lisa soon found herself in the middle of a milling, laughing group, although of course there were the usual irritations of any family Christmas. Helen was already complaining about the boy's behaviour on the drive over, while Sonia was as acid as ever towards Lisa. But after her own erratic childhood, this gossiping, bickering, joking togetherness seemed oddly appealing. If only circumstances had been different, she would have thoroughly enjoyed herself.

She stole a long, troubled look at Matt, who was discussing the share market with his brother-in-law. In spite of all the antagonism and mistrust between them, a familiar, hungry sense of yearning rose inside her. If only things had been different! If only Andrea and Justin hadn't existed. If only Matt hadn't treated them so badly. If only she and Tim hadn't concocted their ridiculous deception! As if Matt felt her eyes on him, he suddenly glanced across at her and for a moment they seemed to be alone in the crowded room. The noise, the laughter, the chinking of glasses spun away and Lisa hung motionless in a void, unable to breathe, unable to do anything but gaze agonizingly at Matt. And then suddenly the spell broke. Colour rushed up into her face and she looked away in confusion, only to find Matt's mother watching them both with a thoughtful expression.

'E-excuse me,' Lisa stammered. 'I must go into the kitchen and see to the dinner.'

The meal went well, everyone agreed on that. The turkey was crisp and brown, oozing with juices, the potatoes were done to perfection, the gravy was tasty and the Christmas pudding, cooked by Judy and reheated by Lisa, was delicious. Only the Brussels sprouts were rather underdone, but nobody complained about that, although Sonia and Helen both left their entire servings on their plates. Otherwise it was a complete success. By the time she was drinking coffee and port and eating far too many chocolates, Lisa felt a glow of triumph. She was really beginning to feel as if she belonged here.

'We're having a barbecue at our place tonight, Lisa,' said Alison, leaning across the table. 'The rest of the family's all coming and we'd be glad if you could join us, too. I'm sure Matt will give you a ride up to Hobart.'

Lisa, who had been on the point of accepting, flinched as if she had been stung. Ride alone with Matt? No, thank you!

'That's really kind of you, Alison,' she said. 'But I'm afraid I can't. I'll be going back to Melbourne as soon as I can get a flight and I've got a lot of packing to do.'

The party began to break up and there was a lot of boisterous kissing under the mistletoe. Tim, who had been drinking champagne liberally, took the opportunity to annoy his mother by hauling Lisa into a passionate clinch.

'Tim, there's no need for such vulgar displays,' said Sonia coldly.

Tim winked and hugged Lisa even harder.

'Oh, don't forget she's soon going to be a member of the family, Mum,' he murmured.

Sonia looked pained, Matt scowled and Patricia and Alison exchanged questioning glances at these cryptic words.

'Matt, are you coming to our barbecue?' broke in Alison.

Matt shrugged. 'I'm not sure,' he growled, momentarily losing his bland manner. 'Don't count on it.'

In the flurry as everyone climbed into their cars, Matt's mother vanished into one of the bedrooms and eventually reappeared and put her arm through Lisa's.

'Tell me, Lisa,' she said. 'There were some Peace roses that I planted when I used to live here. Do you know if they're still growing?'

'Yes, and they're absolutely beautiful,' replied Lisa. 'Shall I cut some for you to take home?'

'If you would, dear.'

She led Lisa off into the secluded corner of the garden where the roses grew and asked her a few questions about her background, saying how much she had enjoyed travelling in the United States herself and telling Lisa that she hoped to see her finished paintings of the Tasman Peninsula soon. Then she pressed a small, rather hastily wrapped package into Lisa's hand.

'A little present for you. It's just something small I had with me, which I wrapped up rather badly in the paper from young William's Nintendo. Matt didn't warn me that you were going to be here, or I would have had a proper gift for you.' She gave an exasperated sigh. 'That's so like him, I'm afraid! He's the dearest man, honest, reliable and loyal, but he's always been dreadfully secretive. Still, I expect there will be other Christmases. Perhaps you'll come and visit me at my home in St Helens one of these days. Well, goodbye, my dear.'

She leaned forward and kissed Lisa on the cheek.

'Thank you,' said Lisa warmly. 'It's really kind of you.'

She didn't realize just how kind it was until she and Matt had finished waving off the guests and were finally left alone in awkward silence.

'What's that?' asked Matt, gesturing to the tiny package in her hand.

'It's a gift from your mother. She said it was just something small she had with her.'

'Why don't you open it?' he demanded.

Lisa did and was appalled. She let out a low gasp.

'Oh, no! I can't possibly take this. It's much too beautiful and expensive. Oh, Matt, look, it's a Tiffany, isn't it?'

She held up the watch made of gold and inlaid with a pattern of lapis lazuli. Matt looked amused.

'Yes, it's Tiffany,' he confirmed. 'She was wearing it when she arrived here. She must have taken it off to give it to you. And she's written you a note, as well. What does that say?'

Lisa opened the hastily scrawled card, scanned through it and groaned. This was even worse!

Dear Lisa,

Tim dropped a rather broad hint that you and Matt will be marrying soon and I must tell you I'll be delighted to welcome you as my daughter-in-law if that happens. I saw from the way you looked at my son how much in love with him you are, although there also seemed to be some trouble between you. Don't let a silly misunderstanding spoil your happiness, I beg you. Make up the difference, whatever it is. Robert and I had so many quarrels, but so many joyful years together. I wish you both the same.

                                    With love,
                                    Patricia Lansdon

A wave of embarrassment and dismay swept over Lisa. No wonder Matt's mother had given her the valuable watch as a present—she thought she was her future daughter-in-law!

'She's got it all wrong,' she exclaimed half hysterically. 'She's completely misunderstood what's going on here! You must give this back to her.'

She tried to thrust the watch at him, but instead of taking it he plucked the note out of her hand.

'Matt, you can't——' she began indignantly.

He ignored her protests and read it through. A brooding expression came into his face.

'Do you really think she's completely misunderstood?' he demanded. 'I've always thought my mother was a very perceptive woman. Lisa, I'm going to ask you a question and I want you to tell me the truth. Are you in love with me?'

Lisa stared at him in torment.

'No! No, I'm not. I won't be, I won't! I don't want to be.'

He caught her in his arms and buried his face in her hair.

'It's not a crime, my love,' he said thickly. 'These things happen. I suppose you thought you could marry Tim for security and then found yourself falling in love with me. But don't fight it, my darling. It's right, it's natural. It's something you should be glorying in. Something we should both be glorying in.'

He kissed her urgently, so that Lisa's head swam at the nearness of him, his spicy, masculine smell, the thrilling pressure of his arms around her. Dizzily she kissed him back, glad that he was supporting her since her legs felt ready to buckle beneath her. Then belatedly she realized how crazy this was and began to struggle against him.

'No, Matt, don't!' she cried, trying to twist free and extricate herself. Her breath was coming in sobbing gasps as if she had been running a marathon. 'We can't do this. There are too many obstacles in our way.'

'Tim?' he demanded with a scornful laugh. 'You're not going to marry Tim, Lisa. I won't stand for it. I'll find a way of stopping you.'

'No, not Tim! What's he got to do with it? I meant Andrea!'

Matt's face was suddenly as stern and cold as a mask. He seized her by the shoulder, gripping her so hard that she cried out.

'Is that what this is about?' he demanded, thrusting his face close to hers. 'About Andrea?'

She nodded mutely and was shocked when he swore under his breath. With a dazed gesture he raised his hand and ran his fingers through his hair then suddenly his eyes focused on hers as sharp and burning as lasers.

'Lisa, trust me!' he urged. 'There is nothing, absolutely nothing between Andrea and me that should cause you a moment's anxiety or guilt. She thinks she's in love with me, but it's pure moonshine and I haven't seduced her or abandoned her, whatever you may think. Do you believe me?'

Lisa stared at him in torment, unsure of whether she could trust him. This wasn't an explanation, just an arrogant demand that she should have blind faith in him. Unhappily she opened her mouth to protest and then paused. Her heart gave an uncomfortable lurch as she realized she did have blind faith in him.

'Yes, I do,' she said in an odd, wondering voice. 'I don't understand what's going on, but I do believe you.'

He gave a growl of triumph low in his throat and hauled her into another crushing embrace.

'Oh, Lisa, Lisa,' he muttered. 'That's all I needed to know. We can sort out all our other problems and nothing else matters. Nothing except that we've found each other and we can give each other so much.'

His kisses rained on her eyelids, her nose, her throat, so that she found herself blinking and gasping, halfway between laughter and tears. Then suddenly he caught her by the arm and began to lead her towards the house.

'Where are you taking me?' she asked breathlessly.

'I think you know that. His voice was nothing but a smoky, seductive vibration. 'I'm going to make love to you, Lisa, and I hope you're not expecting much sleep tonight.'

She had never been in Matt's bedroom before and a tremor of shyness went through her as they came through the doorway. But Matt was so confident, so warm, so protective beside her that her doubts vanished. As he shut the door behind her, she looked around at the carved, four-poster bed with its plaid cover, at the antique furniture and the lace-covered bedside table, lit by a slanting ray of afternoon sun. A hesitant smile curved her lips.

'It's a beautiful room,' she whispered unsteadily, wondering if he could hear the way her heart was thudding against her ribs.

'A beautiful room for a beautiful woman,' he replied, taking both her hands between his as if he intended to warm them.

Lisa felt a sudden, irregular pressure in her palm and looked down. She uttered a soft exclamation of surprise as she realized she was still holding his mother's watch.

'I don't think you need that, do you?' murmured Matt, taking it from her and putting it on the bedside table. 'Or this. Or this. Or these.'

As he spoke he was calmly unfastening her necklace, her dress, her shoes. Lisa found herself sitting on the bed, wearing only a jade silk teddy, while Matt appreciatively peeled off her knickers and tights. Then he began kissing her, starting at her feet and working up her legs.

'Ooh, unfair,' she sighed, wriggling joyously under his touch. You're still dressed.'

'Well, have another Christmas present,' suggested Matt wickedly. 'Unwrap me.'

She obeyed, although her fingers were not quite steady when it came to undoing his shirt and sliding her hands inside to feel his warm, muscular solar plexus. And it was even worse—or better—when she came to undo his belt and the zip of his trousers. In that instant when she saw him naked and fully aroused, her playfulness vanished and was replaced by a dark, throbbing urgency.

'Oh, Matt,' she breathed.

They were standing naked next to the bed and he drew her against him, running his hands over her firm flesh, caressing and exploring every inch of her. Her eyes closed in rapture as his kisses came down over her eyebrows and cheek and across the corner of her lips to the full, ripe centre of her mouth. He kissed her more and more deeply, until they were fused together, their tongues quivering, as a more urgent need overtook them. Lisa felt a dark heat begin to uncoil and pulse deep inside her, and when Matt's hand strayed down and began to stroke her teasingly, she moaned and pressed herself against him. He guided her hand to touch his swollen hardness and she heard him gasp and felt him give a rigid, involuntary shudder of pleasure. An intoxicating sense of power swept over her at the realization that she, too, could make him quiver and sigh and grow tense with desire. Keeping her body pressed against him, she began to sink slowly downwards, wriggling voluptuously so that he felt her breasts and her tossing, luxuriant hair and at last the warm, moist provocation of her mouth upon him.

'Oh, Lisa, you wanton little sex goddess,' he moaned. 'Are you trying to drive me insane? Two can play at that game, you know.'

Gripping her by the hair, he hauled her upright again, treated her to a long, deep, demanding kiss and then lifted her off her feet and dumped her on the bed. After that, with a merciless and utterly blissful thoroughness, he proceeded to show her what he meant. She was aware only of heat, closeness, the rhythmic, maddening, enthralling exploration of each other's bodies. Then a strange sensation began to gather and mass somewhere deep inside her, until she lost all sense of her own separateness and uttered a stifled whimper as wave after wave of ecstatic convulsions shook her to the core.

'Did you enjoy that, my love?' murmured Matt hoarsely. 'Well, there's more to come.'

Still shuddering, with her breath coming in fast, shallow gulps, Lisa found herself crushed into the mattress with his full, hard weight upon her. She inhaled deeply, loving the salty aroma of his skin, the rough hairs on his chest, the grip of his powerful muscles, the length and hardness of him. Loving him. As he lodged himself against her and then drove joyfully inside, her body arched to meet him and she lifted her lips to his cheek, offering small, fluttering kisses until his mouth claimed hers. Their union went on and on. A vigorous, pounding rhythm that fulfilled her utterly so that she smiled mistily up at him, feeling that she wanted to cry. I love you, she thought. I want you to do this to me for years and years and give me babies and have breakfast with me in the mornings and quarrel with me over silly things and love me and love me. And never... ever... leave me.

His eyes were dark and strange and full of secrets, but she sensed the same primitive emotions surging through him. He could not look at her with that intense, brooding possessiveness if he did not love her, could he? And he could not kiss her so fiercely and so tenderly? Or thread his fingers through her hair and frame her face? Or give those deep, labouring sighs as if he could scarcely bear the urgent emotion she aroused in him? Could he? Unless he loved her? Suddenly he caught his breath and stiffened. Then with a low, primal cry he drove deep inside her one final time.

'Oh, Matt, I love you,' she breathed.

He collapsed, sweating and shuddering on top of her, making no reply except to hug her more fiercely against him. But he loved her, too. She was sure of it. A transfiguring joy flooded through her as she nuzzled his face. He hadn't said anything yet about marriage, but Matt Lansdon was a serious, conservative person. Knowing how she felt about him, wouldn't he want to make this union as solemn and binding as possible? Thoughts of white lace and Mendelssohn's wedding march drifted through Lisa's head and she fell asleep.

After a while they woke and made love again. And later they went out and prowled around the wreckage in the kitchen for turkey sandwiches and champagne. Later still they watched television, lying in bed stroking each other. But they didn't really talk, or not about their problems. It was as if the issues of Tim and Andrea were a minefield that they had agreed not to enter, at least for tonight. Instead they kissed and tickled and played hunt the thimble—and other things—under the bedclothes. And somewhere about midnight they both fell asleep.

*   *   *

Lisa awoke shortly after dawn with a deep, aching sense of happiness. She was just coming back from the en suite bathroom when Matt opened the door with a laden breakfast tray in his hands. He sat watching her while she ate toast and bacon and drank orange juice and coffee, then he took the tray from her, set it neatly on the bedside table and scowled at her.

'You're not going to marry Tim, you know,' he announced flatly.

With a sudden lurching sensation in her stomach, Lisa realized that this was the moment she had been waiting for. She would have to tell Matt the truth and clear the air. Only then could their love have a chance to grow and express itself.

'Matt, there's something I want to explain about Tim. You see——'

'There's no need for any explanations,' he cut in harshly. 'I won't pretend it thrills me that you slept with my nephew, but it's better to put the past behind us and never mention it again.'

'But that's the whole point,' she said impatiently. 'I didn't sleep with Tim! I never have done.'

'Don't treat me like a fool, Lisa,' snarled Matt. 'You were stark naked the first time I met you, because you were expecting some kind of extraordinary sexual romp on the dining room table with Tim. How do you explain that? Or how do you explain the fact that Tim told his mother you were planning to marry? Or the way you've been having it off together in that little cottage over the hill from the time Tim arrived here?'

His voice was resonant with anger and outrage, and Lisa could see that whatever Matt said about putting the past behind them, he was still simmering with jealousy and resentment. Would he be relieved or even angrier when she told him how she and Tim had deceived him? Flinching slightly, she took the plunge.

'I can explain it,' she insisted. 'So be quiet and listen. Tim and I never had any intention of marrying. He only told Sonia that because she was throwing a scene about my living in the flat with him.'

Matt gave a short laugh.

'And the fact that you didn't intend to marry but only slept together makes it better?' he demanded. 'I'm afraid I don't agree with that!'

'Will you listen, Matt?' cried Lisa in exasperation. 'I've already told you, I wasn't sleeping with Tim. I've never slept with him. I was only living there quite innocently.'

'Then what exactly were you doing swanning about totally naked, begging him to hurry up and come to you?'

Lisa gave a long, shuddering sigh. 'Oh, help! Tim asked me to keep this secret, but I think I'll have to tell you everything.'

'I think you will,' agreed Matt grimly. 'Go on, then. What were you doing?'

'I was posing for him. Tim's a very talented painter, you know, especially with human figures.'

There was a stunned silence, then suddenly Matt gave a low, sarcastic laugh.

'Really?' he retorted sceptically. 'The day that boy shows a talent for anything other than drinking beer, sleeping in until three in the afternoon and throwing his dirty clothes all over the floor, a miracle will have occurred! Although I must hand him full marks for originality. It's certainly a clever way to get a woman to take her clothes off, telling her he's a painter. But forgive me if I doubt that any painting actually took place.'

'No, I won't forgive you!' shouted Lisa, wrestling herself free of the bedclothes and leaping out of bed. 'You're suspicious and hard and cynical and you don't give poor Tim a chance! You're every bit as bad as he said you were. What's more, you're calling me a liar, aren't you? I'm telling you what really happened between us, which was absolutely zero, and you're flatly refusing to believe me. Well, thanks for your trust.'

Flashing him a burning look, she snatched up her dressing gown and struggled into it, unwilling to let him see her naked any longer. Suddenly Matt seized her arm.

'Wait! This is all pretty unbelievable, Lisa. If what you're saying now is true, why didn't you tell me so that first night in Melbourne?'

'Because Tim wanted to keep our real arrangement secret,' retorted Lisa bitterly.

'Real arrangement? What do you mean by that? The way you bartered your body in return for accommodation?'

'If you say that again, I'll hit you!' threatened Lisa, her voice shaking with rage. 'I didn't barter my body. I bartered painting lessons for accommodation.'

'Painting lessons? You were giving Tim painting lessons?'

'Yes.'

Matt gave a baffled sigh. 'Then why the big mystery about it?'

'Because Tim thought you'd disapprove so strongly that you would stop his allowance and maybe even order him home to the farm. He said he told you he wanted to study art when he finished school, but you refused to listen.'

'Well, how was I supposed to know he was serious about it?' he demanded defensively. 'He never stuck to anything else. Anyway, keep to the point, Lisa. Even if I accept that you were genuinely giving Tim harmless art lessons in exchange for your board, why go on letting me think you intended to marry him? Don't you think you behaved utterly outrageously?'

Lisa flushed guiltily, then her chin came up and she stared Matt straight in the eyes.

'And you offered to buy me off,' she reminded him. 'Without even knowing anything about me, you assumed that I was grasping and manipulative and that I'd stoop to seducing a mere kid. Don't you think you behaved utterly outrageously?'

'That may be so,' he muttered stiffly. 'But it still doesn't explain why you carried the deception so far. Why did you accept my invitation to come here for a visit?'

It was Lisa's turn to look uncomfortable.

'I'm sorry about that. I was so angry that I just rushed into it without thinking. I've always been impulsive, it's my worst fault. You see, I wanted to score off you for humiliating me so badly.'

Matt was still frowning suspiciously. 'It also doesn't explain why you and Tim disappeared off to the cottage so much,' he pointed out. 'I suppose you were posing for him there, too?'

Lisa's eyes blazed dangerously at his sarcasm.

'Yes! As a matter of fact I was! Well, I didn't do much actual posing, except the day when you came down to tell us Sonia had arrived. Mostly what I was doing was just giving him advice. He's been doing an important work for the Buller Art Prize competition.'

'The Buller Art Prize? You must be joking!'

'No, I'm not.'

'But that's a major art prize.'

'I know,' said Lisa proudly. 'And he's short-listed among only four finalists. He's really talented, Matt.'

Matt's eyes narrowed reflectively, but he seemed less interested in his nephew's talent than in something else. Gripping Lisa's shoulders, he looked earnestly at her.

'So you genuinely never slept with him?' he demanded.

She shook her head.

'I wouldn't seduce somebody so young and inexperienced. I take relationships far too seriously for that.'

Matt cupped her face in his hands and gazed at her with an intensity that thrilled and alarmed her.

'I'm relieved to hear it,' he growled. 'If what you're telling me now is true, you've taken a great weight off my mind.'

Leaning down, he kissed her with almost the same reverent sense of purpose as if he was kissing his bride.

'Tim and Sonia will be back soon,' he said with a sigh. 'I suppose it's better if we don't go to bed again just now. Tell me, Lisa, is it possible to view this masterpiece of Tim's?'

'Of course,' she agreed. 'I'll take you down to the cottage and show you.'

Ten minutes later Matt was standing motionless in astonishment before the painting. He was silent for a long, long time, but at last he gave himself a little shake as if he was rousing from a reverie.

'It's superb. I suppose I'll have to give up my opposition to letting the boy study art. Mind you, I'm still going to have plenty to say to him about his slyness and his refusal to face up to me like a man on the issue. Not to mention his impudence in telling Sonia he intended to marry you!'

Matt looked so fierce that Lisa gave a soft giggle as she put her arm around him and led him outside on to the veranda. They were both so intent on each other that they didn't notice a youthful figure hurrying eagerly down the final stretch of road from the other house.

'Don't be too hard on Tim for lying to you about the art lessons and our marriage plans,' begged Lisa, gazing into Matt's eyes. 'He's a nice kid, really, even if he is immature. And there was no malice behind any of it, it was just one of his silly, impetuous schemes.'

At that moment Tim came into view around the Chinese fire bush at the edge of the garden. His face was a study in disbelief and indignation, and it was clear that he had overheard every word she said.

'Thanks for the loyalty, Lisa,' he fumed. 'But where do you get off talking about my silly, impetuous schemes? What about your silly, impetuous schemes? What about your little plot to make Matt fall in love with you, just so you could have the satisfaction of dropping him?'

CHAPTER EIGHT

'WHAT do you mean?' asked Matt in a hushed voice.

His very quietness seemed far more ominous than any shouting would have been, and Tim stepped back a pace, looking uneasy.

'Why don't you ask her?' he retorted, stabbing his finger in Lisa's direction.

'Well, Lisa? Do you have any explanation to offer me?'

The moment Matt's attention was successfully diverted, Tim swerved past them, dashed inside the house and prudently locked the front door, leaving Lisa to deal with the crisis alone. With a sickening sense of apprehension she realized that Matt was far angrier than she had ever seen him before. His eyes were narrowed to mere slits, his nostrils had a curious pinched look and his teeth were gritted in a white line. And in spite of his stillness, she had the sense that he was barely managing to keep himself under control. His hands were clenching and unclenching at his sides, and a muscle was twitching in his cheek.

'Well?' he repeated, thrusting his face within an inch of hers. 'Is Tim telling the truth? Did you plot to make me fall in love with you just so you could have the satisfaction of dropping me? Is that why you slept with me?'

'N-no,' stammered Lisa. 'At least, yes, but not exactly...I mean...'

She backed away in alarm as Matt swore violently under his breath. With a sudden lunge he lashed out, kicking over a terracotta pot of lobelias that stood next to one of the veranda posts. Lisa winced as it shattered loudly, scattering shards of broken pottery along with clumps of dirt and tangled blue flowers. But Matt didn't look at all repentant. He simply stood stock-still, his breath coming in shuddering gulps, staring at the front door where Tim had vanished, as if debating whether to take it off its hinges and smash it to the ground on top of the earthenware pot. Then his gaze swung across to Lisa.

'You unscrupulous little bitch!' he hissed. 'Do you mean to tell me that you slept with me just out of some twisted desire for revenge? Revenge for what?'

Lisa stared at him in horror. Her legs were trembling so violently they would scarcely hold her, and she felt a half hysterical urge to burst into tears. She couldn't believe that everything was going so horribly wrong! If only she hadn't told Tim about that crazy plan of hers! It had been weeks since she had stopped trying to attract Matt just for the sake of revenge. And even if that had still been her only motive, she would never have let it go beyond a mere harmless flirtation. She certainly would never have made love with him for such a despicable reason! How could he possibly believe such a thing of her? At the same time as she was busy blaming herself, a mounting annoyance with Matt began to flare up inside her. Why did he have to leap to such melodramatic conclusions? And anyway, hadn't she had good reason to be annoyed with him in the first place?

'I was angry with you,' she said resentfully. 'I heard you that morning when you were talking on the telephone to Andrea. You told her you were deliberately leading me on so that you could show Tim how fickle I was. You deliberately set out to make a fool of me and humiliate me!'

Matt shut his eyes briefly. When he opened them again they were glinting with hostility.

'And in return for that you were prepared to sleep with me?' he breathed incredulously. 'You were prepared to sigh and murmur and tell me how you loved me just so you could have the pleasure of dumping me a couple of days later? You take my breath away, Lisa. I would never have believed you could stoop so low.'

He turned away from her with a contemptuous expression on his face. Lisa clutched imploringly at his sleeve.

'Matt, it wasn't like that!' she cried. 'I didn't say all those things just to play some rotten trick on you. I really meant them!'

He uttered a mirthless jeer of laughter. 'And you expect me to believe that?'

'Yes. Yes!' she insisted passionately. 'I expect you to believe it, because it's the truth. Look, okay, I did say that stuff to Tim. I did tell him that I was going to try to make you fall in love with me, because I wanted to hurt you and humiliate you just as badly as you had done to me.'

'And I suppose you think you've succeeded now,' sneered Matt.

'No! Of course I don't think I've succeeded. I've wrecked everything! All I ever intended to do was to flirt with you, but instead I fell hopelessly in love with you, because I just couldn't help myself. I love you, Matt. I really do!'

'Do you?' retorted Matt sceptically. 'In that case I suppose it's going to break your heart to hear that I never want to set eyes on you again, Lisa Hayward!'

While she was still staring at him, aghast, he turned and left her.

The sound of the four-wheel drive engine starting up woke Lisa from her paralysis. Choking down the lump in her throat, she dashed after him.

'Matt, wait!'

There was no reply except the indifferent roar of the vehicle as it rushed past her. She caught a brief glimpse of Matt, looking grim and angry as he clenched the steering wheel, then he turned off into the dirt road beyond the gateway. Lisa sprinted after him as hard as she could, but it was nearly a mile from the cottage to the main farmhouse so she had no chance of catching him. The choking dust flung up by the vehicle made her cough, and tiny bits of gravel found their way into her shoes. Ignoring the discomfort, she ran on, and by the time she came stumbling up the last stretch of hillside her breath was coming in burning gulps. She arrived just in time to see that Matt had abandoned the four-wheel drive vehicle in favour of the red Porsche. Lisa stood open-mouthed in dismay as he drove recklessly towards the main road, turned and vanished out of sight.

'Damn,' she breathed. 'Damn, damn, damn! Oh, the brute! How could he?'

Hauling off her shoes, which had been torturing her for the past four hundred metres, she relieved her feelings by flinging them down in the dirt road. Then she burst into tears. Only after she had cried herself to a standstill did she finally pick up the shoes and limp inside the house. In a daze she groped her way into the kitchen and began trying to boil the electric kettle. Perhaps a

cup of tea would make her feel better. Then she thought
of Matt offering her the lemon tea on the cliff top above
Remarkable Cave and her chin began to quiver dangerously again. How ridiculous could she be? Tea wouldn't
help. Nothing would! Her whole life was ruined.

She began to pace restlessly round the kitchen, trying
to make sense of all that had just happened. Well, she
had really made a mess of things this time! She should
never have concocted that silly deception with Tim, nor
hatched her dangerous plan for revenge. But it wasn't
all my fault, a small voice in her head retorted obsti-
nately. What about Matt? He wasn't so pure and
innocent, either. What about telling Andrea he was going
to lead me on to show Tim how faithless I was? Was
that fair? And...Andrea. Oh, heavens! What about
Andrea?

Lisa groaned aloud. It always came back to that. In
the heat of her passion for Matt and her craving to believe that he loved her, had she been wilfully blind to
his faults? Had she convinced herself that he was loyal
and trustworthy when he was really nothing of the kind?
Had he made a fool of her just as thoroughly as Saul
Oakley had done? And if so, how could she ever trust
her own judgment again? Because the fact was that she
had trusted Matt. She couldn't even blame it on her own
youth and naivete this time. She was twenty-five years
old and well aware that there were men in the world who
were unscrupulous predators, trading on their own charm
to lure women into meaningless, degrading affairs. And
yet Matt's voice had had such a ring of truth when he
denied any wrongdoing with Andrea that Lisa had believed him. Now the humiliating possibility that she had
been wrong came sweeping over her. Had she made love
with a man who had only intended to exploit and

abandon her? A man who had never had any deep feelings for her beyond a purely sensual urge to enjoy her body? The thought was unbearable.

But if Matt had only been interested in her body, why had he reacted so violently at the thought that she might merely have been playing games with him? Didn't the intensity of his response imply that he really cared about her? Didn't all that pent-up rage and hurt prove that he loved her? Lisa clung longingly to the idea for a few moments and then shook her head bitterly. Not necessarily, she told herself. It might have been nothing but masculine pride. There are plenty of men who think it's fine to play games with women, who don't like having the same thing done to them. The truth is that I have no idea what Matt's real feelings are towards me and I was a fool ever to let things go so far between us without knowing that. Oh, I wish he'd come back just so that I could get all this sorted out. I can't bear this uncertainty!

Her glance strayed to the kitchen clock and she let out a worried sigh. It was more than half an hour now since Matt had driven away. Where had he gone? What was he doing? When would he come back? And then she remembered that night in the cabin at Fortescue Bay. Faced with an explosive, emotional situation he had rushed off then, too, and only returned when he was completely under control. Well, perhaps he would do the same thing now. But even if he did come back looking cool and glib and imperturbable, she would find some way of breaching his armour! Somehow they must talk about what had happened between them. Even if they were going to part—and the mere thought sent a stab of pain like a knife wound through her heart—then she needed to understand what was going on. She must wait until he came back and then make him talk to her.

When the kitchen door swung open behind her, her heart almost stopped beating. Gazing sightlessly down at her hands, she realized that she had been shredding a paper napkin and plaiting it into tiny braids. Clutching at it as if it was a lifeline, she turned slowly and moistened the roof of her mouth with her tongue.

'Matt——' she began.

But it was not Matt. It was a jaunty, boyish figure, who darted only one brief, sheepish glance at her before launching into speech.

'Oh, hi, Lisa. Listen, have you seen the ball of twine or the little box of tacks anywhere? Or that small hammer? I need to crate up my painting.'

Lisa's only response was to give Tim a burning look, then stride through the kitchen to the laundry. She returned a moment later with her arms full and proceeded to open a box of tacks and pour them out on the floor in front of him. After that, she coiled off length after length of twine from the ball before flinging it in his face. Finally she dropped the hammer right on his feet.

'Ouch!' exclaimed Tim, jumping back a moment too late. 'You're upset about something, aren't you, Lisa?'

'What ever gave you that idea?' choked Lisa.

And flinging herself down at the table she buried her face in her hands and burst into tears again.

Tim was appalled. He looked longingly at the door, fell on one knee to pick up the hammer and a few of the tacks and then evidently thought better of it. Dropping them again on the floor, he came over and put his hands awkwardly on Lisa's shoulders.

'What's wrong, Lisa?' he asked.

'Everything!' she replied unsteadily. 'You've wrecked everything, telling Matt that I was only trying to get revenge on him. It wasn't true any more. I really had fallen in love with him.'

'Fallen in love with him?' echoed Tim incredulously. 'You mean...my uncle Matt?'

'Yes.'

'But he's a brute,' protested Tim. 'Overbearing, strict, a killjoy.'

'I know,' wailed Lisa. 'But I love him. And now he's left me.'

Alarmed by the threat of further tears, Tim picked up the ruined napkin and dabbed at her face with it.

'What's this? Have you taken up macramé?'

Lisa gave a watery giggle and allowed Tim to hug her.

'Look, I'm sorry I dumped you in it with Matt,' he said. 'I lost my temper when I heard you calling me immature. I've always been very mature for my age.'

That made Lisa give another smothered giggle and in a moment she felt recovered enough to return Tim's hug. Looking relieved, he straightened up and slouched across to the kettle.

'Would you like a cup of tea?' he asked.

'Tim! I don't think you've ever made me a cup of tea in all the time I've known you.'

'Well, if you have ambitions to be my aunt by marriage I suppose I'd better take care of you, you poor old bat.'

'Old bat!' cried Lisa indignantly, but she accepted the cup.

'Is that your ambition?' asked Tim. 'To marry Matt?'

'I don't know,' she said huskily. 'If I felt sure that Matt loved me, yes, nothing would make me happier. But I'm not sure of anything any more.'

'Have you slept with him?'

Lisa blushed and then nodded. Tim gave a soft whistle.

'Then you really are serious about him! Did he tell you what he felt about you?''

Her face shadowed. 'Not exactly,' she admitted at last. 'But from the way he was behaving I thought he must love me. Then I started to think about Andrea, and I wasn't sure any more. Tim, do you think Matt really is Justin's father?'

'I don't know,' Tim said with a perplexed sigh. 'It's hard to see how it can be anybody else, especially seeing how much the kid looks like him. And there's the fact that Matt knows about the rumours and doesn't try to stop them. All the same, it doesn't seem like him to leave Andrea in the lurch, even if he didn't love her. He's always so gung ho about responsibility! But if he did do that to her, maybe you're better off without him.'

'That's what I keep telling myself but I don't feel it. Deep down I don't believe it. I wish he'd come back and explain it all to me.'

'He probably will eventually,' said Tim. 'Of course he must have been really upset to rush off like that. I've never seen him look so dangerous before. But he's got to come home sooner or later.'

Yet after another half hour there was still no sign of Matt, and Tim was beginning to grow restive. Lisa was just about to take pity on him and send him down to crate up the painting when the door opened. Lisa half rose from her seat and slumped back in disappointment. It was only Judy Barwick!

'Hello,' she said cheerfully. 'Had a nice Christmas? Tell me, what's all this about your uncle Matt jetting off to Hong Kong?'

'Hong Kong?' chorused Tim and Lisa in shocked tones.

'Yes, didn't he tell you? He rang me at home a few minutes ago and said he'd decided to go away indefinitely. Some business trip, I suppose. Or perhaps he just felt that he needed a break.'

A week later Lisa was kneeling on the floor of her bedroom in the flat in Melbourne with an array of half-packed suitcases and boxes around her. She had a headache and her eyes felt swollen and scratchy, but that was nothing new. She had been feeling that way ever since she and Tim flew out of Tasmania. Tim had turned out to be surprisingly kind once they both realized that Matt wasn't going to return. In addition to packing up his painting, he had packed up Lisa with almost equal tenderness. Faced with her distraught condition, which was quite beyond his understanding, he had treated her as if she was a very young child. Organizing her bags, driving her to the airport, urging her to eat her snack on board the plane. And after delivering his painting to the judges, he had even offered to come home and keep her company. But company was the last thing Lisa wanted right now. When Tim finally accepted this, he left with obvious relief in search of Barbara. Apart from a brief phone call—'Lisa? I'm at the beach house in Portsea if you need me'—Lisa hadn't heard from him all week.

Just as well, really, she thought with a sigh. She was still very fond of Tim, but there was no denying that his presence reminded her of many things she would rather forget. Besides, she didn't want to infect him with her gloom, when he was so full of high spirits about the prospect of going to study in Paris. And he would only be in the way while she was packing. He had tried to persuade her to stay on in the flat indefinitely, but Lisa had been immovable on that issue. The place belonged to Matt and there was no way her pride would let her go on living there even if she never set eyes on Tim's uncle again. Besides, Matt might want to let the place out to a genuine tenant, if Tim did go overseas to study.

Well, there was no point sitting here brooding! She must get on with tossing out a few more crumpled sketches and find all the odd socks that seemed to be missing from her drawers. She was just dumping out her underwear drawer on the bed when the doorbell rang. For a moment Lisa froze, with a wild hope thudding in her chest, then she forced herself to take a deep, calming breath. Don't be stupid, she thought. Tim's probably come up to town with Barbara and forgotten to bring his key. But it wasn't Tim who was standing on the front doorstep. It was Matt.

He looked just as suave and well groomed as ever in lightweight grey slacks and a striped blue and white shirt. As usual his face gave nothing away, but Lisa was annoyed to feel the old, familiar lurch of excitement at the mere sight of him. Instinctively she gave ground and stepped back a pace or two, looking at him nervously. Matt promptly took advantage of her retreat to step calmly inside and close the front door behind him.

'Any chance of some coffee?' he asked.

Coffee? Why on earth did he want coffee? This request seemed as bizarre to Lisa as if it had been made while she was in the midst of fleeing for her life from a tidal wave or a volcanic eruption or some other natural disaster. Yet the force of Matt's personality mesmerized her.

'I suppose so,' she said unsteadily and turned to lead the way upstairs.

Once in the kitchen she switched on the percolator and the normality of the surroundings helped to steady her nerves a little. Why had he come? What did he want? But Matt showed no sign of wanting anything. He strolled casually into the dining room and was looking around it approvingly.

'It's much tidier than it was the first time I met you,' he remarked.

Colour flooded into Lisa's face at the reminder.

'Yes, I cleared away all the paints and brushes,' she muttered. 'I suppose Tim and I should never have used it as a studio without your consent, but I don't think anything's been damaged. Look, I'll go and get the coffee.'

She sidled out of the room and returned a few minutes later with a tray. Matt rose to his feet and came towards her.

'Forget the coffee!'

'Why are you here?'

They both spoke together and to Lisa's ears it sounded like the salvo of gunfire at the start of a war. She heard the cups rattle as she set down the tray and realized that she had made no progress at all in feeling indifferent towards him.

'Why are you here?' she repeated bitterly.

Matt gave a harsh laugh.

'If I told you I couldn't stay away, would that be an adequate answer?'

'No.'

'Then what if I tell you that Tim phoned me and said you were going to pieces with misery?'

'Tim phoned you?' she echoed. 'How could Tim phone you? Judy told us you were in Hong Kong!'

'They have telephones in Hong Kong.'

Lisa stared at him in disbelief. 'And you came back here because of that?' she demanded.

'Is it really so unlikely?' He took a step closer. 'Is it true, Lisa? Are you miserable?'

'No,' she choked.

'So your red eyes and pale face are just a sign that you've been out on the tiles enjoying yourself, are they? I must say you look as if you're pretty ecstatic.'

'Stop tormenting me!' flared Lisa and then gasped as he gripped her by the shoulders.

'You're the one who's tormenting me,' he corrected. 'Lisa, Tim also swears that you really are in love with me. I've got to know...is that true?'

She took a long, shuddering breath.

'What does it matter? Why do you want to know? You're still collecting trophies, are you?'

Matt swore under his breath.

'I never have collected trophies! I never will. All right, I admit that there were other women in my life before I met you, but they were only ever women that I respected and liked. And when we parted it was mutual.'

Lisa thought of Andrea and her lips twisted sceptically.

'Was it?' she asked.

'Yes, it was! Look, Lisa, never mind the other women in my life, all that's over and finished. What I want to talk about is us. I want to know what you feel for me now.'

'I don't feel anything for you!' she retorted and was annoyed that she could not keep the tremor out of her voice.

'Don't lie to me,' he snarled. 'That's as meaningless as it would be for me to say I don't feel anything for you.'

'Well, you don't!' cried Lisa. 'You never liked me, right from the beginning.'

She heard Matt's harsh intake of breath.

'That's not entirely true,' he said. 'I disapproved of you in the beginning, but I was violently attracted to you from the very start.'

Lisa thrust down an unwelcome thrill of pleasure at that revelation.

'Oh, yes? So attracted to me that you called me an ambitious little schemer?'

'Well, what was I supposed to call you?' he demanded savagely. 'You let me believe that you were sleeping with Tim and planning to marry him, didn't you? I didn't know whether it was for love or money, but you very soon admitted to me that love didn't come into it. So was I supposed to admire your fine character?'

Lisa glared at him. 'And what about your fine character?' she retorted. 'You tried to buy me off, didn't you?'

Matt winced. 'Yes, and it didn't work. That's when I had my first suspicion that money wasn't really important to you, after all. Still, it was always possible that you were simply playing for even higher stakes. When you burnt my cheque, I was furious. I was even more furious to find that it made me even more violently attracted to you than before.'

'And that's why you kissed me in the lift at the State Theatre?'

'Yes. And that was a mistake. You were sheer dynamite, Lisa! I've never been so aroused by a woman in my entire life. I was outraged to think that my callow young nephew could succeed with you where I couldn't, so I vowed that I was going to have you.'

Lisa looked at him with unwilling interest as a swarm of questions began to buzz in her head.

'Did you deliberately scheme to get Tim left behind in Melbourne?' she asked.

Matt gave a throaty growl of laughter.

'Yes,' he admitted. 'I didn't think he'd be able to resist the temptation to escape. And he didn't.'

'And I suppose you thought that once you got me alone I'd jump into bed with you?' cried Lisa indignantly.

Matt had the grace to look ashamed.

'Something like that,' he muttered. 'But it didn't work out the way I expected. You turned out to be much nicer than I thought you would be. You also seemed to have scruples about things that wouldn't have bothered you if you were a genuine gold-digger. Like paying for your own airline ticket. And then I found that something really alarming was happening to me.'

'What do you mean?'

'I was beginning to like you. I began to wonder if I'd misjudged you, but at the same time I was deeply uneasy. I decided I'd try to find out the truth about you. If you really were a mercenary little bitch, I told myself I'd be doing Tim a favour by exposing what you really were. If you weren't, then . . . I'd have to reassess the situation. All I knew for sure was that I wanted to make you fall for me.'

'So if I hadn't overheard you talking to Andrea, would you really have lured me into bed with you just to show Tim how fickle I was?' demanded Lisa indignantly.

Matt winced.

'I don't know. I wasn't thinking terribly clearly and most of what I was thinking was pure self-deception anyway. I tried to kid myself that what I was doing was just to save Tim from your clutches, but that wasn't true at all. The real reason I wanted you to fall for me is that you intrigued me so much. I wanted you to lie awake at night aching for me the way I did for you.'

'Well, you succeeded,' said Lisa dryly. 'I did love you desperately and I was really beginning to fall under your spell until I heard what you said to Andrea. It's because you had conned me so successfully that I felt so furious when I realised that it was all just an underhanded plot.'

'And you dreamt up your own underhanded plot for revenge?'

Lisa nodded bleakly.

'Well, you really turned the tables on me,' growled Matt. 'Although it was a stroke of luck for you that Tim arrived when he did.'

'Luck, nothing!' jeered Lisa. 'I phoned him in Melbourne and blackmailed him into coming down to Tasmania. Then we agreed to pretend that we were sleeping together.'

'You really know how to hurt a man, don't you?'

'Were you hurt?'

'I was so jealous that I was seriously tempted to knock Tim down, drag you off by the hair, fling you onto my bed and ravish you. You were driving me insane with desire.'

'Well, you drove me fairly insane with desire at Fortescue Bay,' she told him.

Matt gave her a long, searching look.

'Why did you beg me not to make love to you there?' he asked. 'You told me that you were afraid that you'd lose your self-respect. I thought you were talking about your engagement to Tim and I admired you for it. But that doesn't make sense, does it? You never did sleep with Tim, did you?'

Lisa shook her head.

'No,' she agreed huskily. 'I don't know why I'm telling you this, Matt, especially when you've never been completely open with me. But I suppose I might as well tell you the truth. Up until that moment in the cottage at Fortescue Bay I kept trying to convince myself that I could play my silly game of revenge without getting burnt. That I could stop whenever I wanted. Then that night I realised I was in love with you.'

'In love with me? But you wouldn't let me make love to you. That doesn't make sense.'

'Yes, it does!' insisted Lisa passionately. 'I was in love with you, but I thought you were just playing games with me. And I was so upset by what you'd done to Andrea. How could I trust myself to a man like that?'

'Yet you did trust yourself to me a few weeks later,' he reminded her.

She nodded miserably and felt her eyes prickle with sudden tears.

'More fool me!' she said savagely.

'Why did you?' demanded Matt, gripping her shoulders. 'Why did you, Lisa? Was it just to get your revenge?'

'No!' she cried, twisting away from him. 'Don't be a fool, Matt! I did it because I loved you, because I trusted you, in spite of what you'd done to Andrea.'

'I've never done anything to Andrea!' he snapped.

She stared at him in disbelief. 'But Justin——'

'Justin is not my child! I've never made love to Andrea in my life.'

A wild surge of elation swept over her, followed by immediate uneasiness. 'Everybody says——'

'I know what they say! It isn't true. Justin is not my child.'

'Then whose——'

'My cousin Graham's.' He saw her baffled frown, and his grip on her shoulders suddenly grew gentler, almost caressing. 'Sit down, Lisa, and I'll explain.'

Wonderingly she sank into a chair and watched as he paced across to the huge picture window.

'Graham and I were only a year apart,' he said. 'And we were really close to each other, more like brothers than cousins. We also looked very much alike. He married young, but the marriage wasn't happy, and eventually he started having an affair with a schoolteacher.'

'Andrea?' whispered Lisa.

'Yes. Andrea. When Graham was lost at sea, Andrea was already pregnant, and she was absolutely distraught to hear the news. I did my best to help her, and a lot of people leapt to the conclusion that Justin was my child. Under the circumstances, it seemed cruel to Graham's widow to reveal the truth. So I let them go on thinking it. The trouble was that, as time passed, Andrea convinced herself that she was in love with me, but I'm sure it's not true. It's just an infatuation, based on the fact that I look like Graham. One of these days she'll meet someone else and snap out of it.'

'Now I understand,' murmured Lisa, half to herself. 'Oh, Matt. And you're not in love with her?'

He turned with his back against the window like an animal at bay and faced her.

'How could I be?' he asked. 'When I'm totally and absolutely in love with you?'

There was such a driven look in his eyes, so much need and longing and resentment and hope that Lisa gave a stifled cry, jumped to her feet and ran to him. His arms closed around her and he crushed her against him so hard that she could feel the violent beating of his heart against her cheek.

'Truly?' she faltered.

'Truly,' he said thickly. 'Lisa, I've got a few suggestions to make.'

'Mm?'

'Why don't you finish your packing and come back to Tasmania with me? I'll buy the farm from Tim and we can go and visit him in Paris on our honeymoon.'

A radiant burst of happiness spread through her limbs like a sunrise.

'That sounds fine to me,' she whispered.

An equal flare of triumph and joy blazed in Matt's eyes. He hugged her hard, then reached up and tugged sharply at the cord beside the window so that the Austrian blinds dropped down, shutting out the light. After that he began calmly unbuttoning Lisa's blouse.

'We've been apart for too long,' he murmured into her ear. 'Why don't we celebrate our reunion by making violent love all over the flat? Starting with the dining room?'

She swayed against him, purring like a cat. A slow, delicious smile curved her lips.

'Yes, why not?' she agreed.

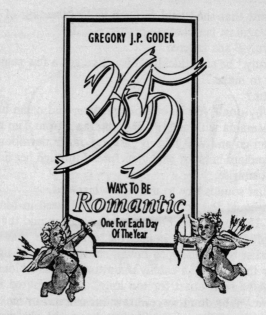
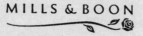

A year's supply of Mills & Boon Romances—absolutely FREE!

Would you like to win a year's supply of heartwarming and passionate romances? Well, you can and they're FREE! Simply complete the wordsearch puzzle below and send it to us by 30th June 1996. The first 5 correct entries picked after the closing date will win a years supply of Mills & Boon Romances (six books every month—worth over £100). What could be easier?

READER SERVICE
ROMANCE
RESIST
HEART
MEMORIES
PAGES
KISS
SPINE
TEMPTATION
LOVE
COLLECTION
ROSES
PACK
PARCEL
TITLES
DREAMS
COUPLE
SPECIAL EDITION
EMOTION
DESIRE
SILHOUETTE
MOODS
PASSION

M	E	R	O	W	A	L	R	L	M	S	P	C	O	S
	O		E	C	I	V	R	E	S	R	E	D	A	E	R
R	O					E		O	S	M	A	E	R	D	S
O	D	H	E	A	R	T		S		S		S	E	L	T	I	T
M	S				S		E		M	E	M	O	R	I	E	S	S
A	E				C	G			S	A		C				E
N	P	T			A		E	K		W		O	I			W
C	E		T	P	K	I	S	S	C			L	T	T		O
E				E		H		A	E	V	O	L		E	N	N
	A	E		U		M		P	R		T	E	I	M	O	E
	E	N		L	O			L	I		S	C		P	I	O
S	L	I			H	A		S		I	T		T	S	A
	P	P	A	R	C	E	L	N	E		S	I		A	S	Z
	U	S	D	B			I	D		E	O		T	A	I
O	O		O		N			B	S		R	N		I	P	S
	C		E	N	N	A	M	T	R	R	L	G	N	O	L	T
	O		E	M	O	T	I	O	N			O		N		I
N	O	I	T	I	D	E	L	A	I	C	E	P	S	K

Please turn over for details of how to enter...

How to enter

Hidden in the grid are words which relate to our books and romance. You'll find the list overleaf and they can be read backwards, forwards, up, down or diagonally. As you find each word, circle it or put a line through it.

When you have found all the words, don't forget to fill in your name and address in the space provided below and pop this page into an envelope (you don't need a stamp) and post it today. Hurry—competition ends 30th June 1996.

Mills & Boon Wordsearch
FREEPOST
Croydon
Surrey
CR9 3WZ